# THE DAIRY MAIDS AND THE HIRED MAN

The Complete Collection

---

## LACY TATE

# Copyright

Join Lacy's blog to find out about new Manley Dairy stories, where lusty, busty, milky women lactate for everyone's delectation.

Kenny, Part One

————————————

KENNY HELD his Stetson by the brim, crushing another dent into it. His potential boss, dairy owner Dirk Manley, sat across the kitchen table piled with stacks of letters and printouts. One very tall stack, one much shorter. He read through Kenny's credentials.

That last horse that kicked him in the ribs might just have changed his career at twenty-four, though Kenny'd grown up on a farm and planned to make it his life. The Manley Dairy's ad for "Farm work, light lifting, high pay for the right applicant" sounded too good to be true. Guess a whole lot of guys thought the same. The fields and pastures around the farmhouse looked like a regular farm, but he'd seen a lot more outbuildings close to the house than he could account for, swarming with men and women who didn't look like farmers.

Kenny eyed the man who held his fate in his hands. Early forties, six feet plus some, broad shoulders, tanned. Too good looking to stay on the farm, but said he'd never done anything else, although his produce was, ah, how did Mr. Manley put it? Eclectic. Probably meant pygmy cattle. Damn, that meant stooping to milk.

"Your farming skills check out, Kenny, but we have one more set of interviews for you. At this dairy, you won't get far if you don't meet with the approval of my Dairy Maids. They have their own criteria for hiring, which is, heh, a little different from mine." Dirk grinned. "Please them and you could have a long and happy career here."

"Sounds good, sir." Dairy maids? Maybe he wouldn't have to bend over to milk miniature cows. "When do I meet the ladies?"

"Soon. Your tasks will include regular milkings and application of pro-milk stimulants, and if the Dairy Maids don't like you, you won't last. But you seem like a personable young man."

"I get along with most everyone, sir." What was so tough about these dairy maids? Kenny followed his potential boss into the parlor of the old farm house, to set with what had to be three other would-be hired men. All good looking, one with a shit-eating grin on his face, one with a magazine in his hands that couldn't be that interesting upside down. They didn't make room for Kenny on the brocade Victorian couch. The third sat silently on a hard-backed chair with his hat on his knee. Kenny took another such chair. All the applicants looked fit and strong. Kenny hoped his lingering injury didn't put him out of the running. Being a hair over six feet tall with light brown hair, hazel eyes and strong, regular features had never helped him with the chores, but if he needed the dairy maids to like him, he supposed he looked good enough even in this company.

"Come in, my dear Dairy Maids!" Dirk boomed at the front door.

A crowd of women in white blouses and blue skirts of all shades giggled their way into the parlor. My goodness gracious fucking A, this was a fine looking group! Blondes, brunettes, a redhead, one imposing black woman with a thousand long braids. Some thin, some curvy, and every last one of them with enormous tits.

Where in the hell had Dirk Manley found so much gorgeousness willing to work in a dairy? Please don't let them be divas. And please let one or two of them be willing to fraternize with the hired man. Kenny'd never wanted to work anywhere so much in his entire life.

All four men hit their feet, hats in hand.

"Well, well, well, looky what we have here!" exclaimed the black woman. "Time for some inter-viewing for sure!" She surveyed them, and Kenny knew who ran the dairy maids. "Let's see now, Mindy,

Rita, you take this fella upstairs and give him the low-down on the job." She pointed at the silent sitter. "You gwan now, see if you and the dairy suit each other."

That was fast. Why did the sour guy get picked first? The redhead, who wore dark blue, and one brunette in light blue escorted him to the carved staircase, and upstairs. Who would Kenny get to be alone with, and where? He glanced past them at Dirk, who just gave a little salute and left them to the mercies of the ladies.

"So who do we have here?" Now she gave names and asked them. "I'm India, here's Chelle, Kitty, Emily, Amy, and Taylor."

Kenny struggled to remember which name went with which woman, but his big head swam and his little head was getting way too hard to think. He kept his hat over his groin.

"Chelle and Emily, you take Brett here. Taylor, Amy, you get Kenny, and Travis, you come with me and Kitty. Think we can all get along?" India might have smiled but Kenny was having a rugged time noticing anything but her tits.

Footsteps thudded down the staircase.

Sourpuss paused at the front door long enough to yell, "These women are fucking crazy! I'm out of here!" The door slammed behind him, and a pickup truck's roar followed.

One of the blondes *tsk'd.* "We really shouldn't let Rita interview."

The two women came downstairs more slowly, and the redhead waved on their way out the door.

India *hmphed.* "Didn't think he'd last long anyway." Taking the arm of the grinner, she said, "Kitty and I will assess ol' Travis's suitability for the Dairy, down by the hickory grove."

"We'll show Brett the barn," said one of the blondes, and the nervous reader was escorted out.

That left Kenny with a lovely blonde of about five foot eight and a brunette somewhat shorter. What kind of crazy could these ladies be? He tried desperately to maintain eye contact. Which was which? "Howdy, Miss Amy, Miss Taylor."

"I'm Amy," said the blonde in a dark blue skirt. "Don't be nervous. We're not really crazy." She smiled, and his cock got harder. "Rita's just a bitch."

"We could go upstairs and chat," suggested Taylor, who looked just as friendly as Amy, and dressed nearly the same, though her skirt was lighter. Medium blue gingham should flip up just as well as dark blue did.

Kenny tried to drag his thoughts out of the gutter. "Maybe we should stay here and chat?"

Amy gave the hard couch and the pileless carpet an assessing glare. "Um, no." She took Kenny's arm, and led him to the staircase.

If the important thing was keeping these lovelies happy, upstairs he would go. And do his damnedest to stay polite, when all he could think of was pushing his face between their tits and motorboating fit to drive a supertanker.

Damn but they were fucking with his resolve by leading him to a bedroom! How the hell was he supposed to maintain when the only piece of furniture fit to sit on was a king-sized bed? If they didn't take his hat away, he could lean against the wall and they could sit.

Amy shut the door. Kenny swallowed hard, trying to remove the boulder that suddenly clogged his throat.

Taylor took his arm and batted her big brown eyes at him. "Now, how much did Dirk tell you about this job?"

The boulder needed another two swallows before he could get words out, because Amy clung to his other arm and regarded him just as warmly.

"Uh, that this was a very productive dairy, and that I needed to get along with my dairy maid colleagues, and that I would be milking and, um…" How had Dirk phrased that? "Applying pro-milk stimulants. Which I hope you'll tell me about, because I've only worked on organic farms and never gave the cows anything like that."

"Oh, we're organic all right," Amy purred, stroking his arm in a very distracting way. "And you won't have to use nasty chemicals."

"Our cows get the best treatment, good food, sunshine, frequent milkings," Taylor agreed. "They produce marvelous milk. They don't need pro-milk stimulation."

Stimulation was a dirty word for Kenny right now, because two of the most delicious girls he'd ever met were crowding him hard enough to press their enormous titties against his arms. His cock strained inside his jeans.

"I don't understand. It sounds like hormones." Hormone-laden milk was getting harder to sell, he knew.

"It is. All natural though." Taylor giggled.

"Don't you produce a lot of milk?" This job had sounded like he'd be washing udders and attaching milkers.

"Oh yes, we do." Amy giggled and rubbed her breasts harder against his arm. "Except you mean 'you, the dairy' and it should be 'you, the dairy maids.' Kenny, Taylor and I are the ones who need the hormones, and it's wonderful men who provide them for us."

"Buh…" Kenny's brain shorted out entirely. Anything he guessed right now would be too good to be true and insult the very people he needed to get along with. "Ladies, why don't you just teach me what I need to know about this job?"

"That's the spirit!" Amy pulled his head down for—a kiss? He met her parted lips hesitantly, and then more firmly when he realized she meant this, she wanted his mouth on hers. Busty little Taylor wiggled with anticipation, smushing her titties against his arm. He bent to kiss her, too, and wrapped his arm around her shoulders.

If he creamed his jeans now… No, no, no. "I do try to be a good worker, Miss Amy." A little formality and he'd back away from the brink.

"Excellent!" She batted her blue eyes and her lashes seemed long enough to tickle his cock from there. "We'll start with the milking. Sometimes we need equipment. Right now, we'll do it by hand."

"So to speak." Taylor's giggles had dropped an octave. "Like this."

The dairy maids let go of his arm, which made Kenny's heart sink, until he saw—they were pulling their white blouses down! The crisp white cotton of their shirts stretched a long way to expose four huge, firm, lace-covered breasts. His eyes bugged out almost as far as their busts.

"But of course you can't get any milk until we're bare." Amy opened a clasp between those luscious mounds, and the pink lace cups sighed apart. She uncovered her huge tits. "You'll get the hang of this pretty fast."

God damn, but Kenny would be the fastest learner on the planet. Truly melon-sized and creamy white, Amy's breast stood proud on her chest, offered in her willing hand. Kenny licked his lips. "If that other guy turned down anything like this, he was the crazy one."

"If you're still standing there while I'm offering, you're a bit crazy too." Amy pinched her nipple, her stiff, rosy nipple. Drops of white formed on her peak, to fall away when they grew too large to cling to her flesh.

Her nipple was dripping. Dripping milk. Amy was dripping milk from her enormous titty, and he was standing here like a fool. "Not crazy, just… a little unsure." His cock didn't have any doubts though, and he had to rearrange himself inside his pants before he broke in two. Thank goodness for the hat.

"Is it big?" Taylor noticed—hiding behind his Stetson hadn't helped. "That's important."

"Gets the job done," Kenny choked out. The size of his dick was a job requirement? He'd let them decide if seven thick inches was big enough. "Want to see?"

"Milk first," Amy announced. "I'm waiting." She sat back on the bed, her knees apart.

"Don't stand there, get to milking," Taylor pushed him toward her friend. "She's very full, and I'm getting fuller by the minute."

Get to… okay, who was he to argue? Kenny dropped to his knees before her. He tried cupping her breast between both hands and squeezing. Milk flew in a fine spray mixed with ropy streams. Her breast spurted milk, like… he didn't want to say like a cow's teats, not aloud. "You're milking!"

"No, I'm lactating, you're supposed to be milking,"

Amy corrected him, though she let him press more milk out. His face grew wet from the spray. "We can splosh later if you like, but right now you're supposed to be milking me."

"Oh… oh…What?" Kenny stopped squeezing and trying to catch drops with his tongue. "What am I doing wrong?" Would she make him let go?

Far from it. With a gentle hand on the back of his head, she guided him to her nipple.

"Open wide, now, take a big mouthful of me. This isn't like sex—"

"Yes, it is," interrupted Taylor, who sat next to pretty blonde Amy, the better to supervise. "Well, milk first."

There might be milk, but that was a marvelous tit right in front of his face. Kenny reached out with his tongue to lick the rosy nub poking toward him.

"Don't listen to her. Just suckle me, Kenny." Amy sighed when his tongue touched her nipple. "Milk will make you big and strong."

The milk had already made him big: his dick needed another quick shift inside his jeans. "Yes, Ma'am," he said, but not until he'd swiped his tongue over her areola, finding it was all crinkly on his second pass around. But he did as he was told and wrapped his lips around her bud and sucked his first taste of Amy's milk.

Oh fuck but her tit was huge, and full! He barely had to suck after the first few mouthfuls—her creamy goodness squirted into his mouth after the first few swallows. More and more sprayed out of her, just for the pressing. He wanted to moan for the warmth and the taste, thin and sweet but getting thicker every few swallows. Not letting go of her breast meant he could cup all that amazing flesh with both hands. Kneading and playing, he discovered he could help her let down. Careful though, he might get enough to drown. Fuck but she was full!

"Oh nice," Amy sighed, running her fingers through his short brown hair. "Keep doing that."

Oh, he would, he would, Kenny'd do anything that might make this woman fall backward with her legs open. Or maybe she'd let him rub his cock between those milk jugs. Or his face. Or both. All at once. If that was possible. Maybe if Taylor helped…

He thought he'd suckle until he passed out or came in his pants, but after a good long drink, enough to quench his thirst, he found her gushes slowing to squirts and spurts. Her flow slowed to a trickle, and he had to work her with his hands for the last swallows. Nice, it was getting like sex again.

"Enough, Kenny, that side's drained." Amy dropped a kiss on his head. "Like it?"

He released her reluctantly and with a kiss to the still-hard nipple. "Miss Amy, that was the most amazing drink I ever had." Better than his first bourbon and Seven, better than cold water on a hot day. He'd just drunk, holy fuck, he'd just drunk milk from a woman's breast. And there was nothing babylike about him at all, no sirree, not with the raging monster in his pants that needed to plunge into the honey depths between her legs.

"Then you'll like the other side just as much," she declared.

Taylor giggled, clutching Amy's arm. "Try to remember what it tastes like, so you can compare sides and then compare mine."

Hers. Compare. He'd have to taste. More tits. He'd have to taste more tits. Drink more milk. "Miss Taylor, I can safely say this is like no job interview I've ever done." He buried his face into Amy's breasts and hoped no one would tap his shoulder to say, "Wake up."

Amy giggled. "We have to know if you're willing to suckle. Not everyone is." She pressed her ginormous titties to his cheeks.

"I'm willing! I'm willing!" Just in case she might take her breasts away, Kenny captured her as-yet-unsucked but dripping nipple between his lips. "Mmm…"

Oh fuck—he'd always been a tit man, and only in his wildest fantasies had luscious ladies lactated for him. Now two—two of how many?—beautiful, milky women wanted him to suckle at their nipples. He stole a glance at Taylor, whose lacy peach cups showed tall bumps and dark spots over them. Damn, she was letting down just watching them! Her blue eyes were wide and her lips were parted, and she reached out to stroke his shoulder.

Oh, both of them wanted him to suck at Amy's tits! With every mouthful his dick throbbed. What other of their fluids would they share with him?

Amy liked what he was doing—a woman didn't catch her breath nor ease her seat like that if she didn't. Was he doing her well enough to be asked to stay? Kenny lashed his tongue across her flowing nipple, to taste, to please her, to make her smile. To make her take him all the way between her thighs. Her milk flowed thick and creamy now, so sweet and rich. Greedy for every drop, Kenny nuzzled and rolled her luscious milk across his taste buds. He almost hated to swallow—the milk would disappear down his gullet. But more flowed. And more.

Finally even his best efforts brought only droplets. Amy soothed his loss. "There'll be more. You have to wait a bit. Did you like that?"

Did she need to ask? "Miss Amy, that was so wonderful, I don't even have words." Kissing her breasts would have to make his appreciation plain. Damn, nothing about this woman's breasts could be tamed by two lone hands!

"I'd say we're sure he's willing to suckle," Amy murmured, her arms around Kenny's shoulders. Oh, fuck yeah, she wasn't pushing him away. "Wouldn't you agree, Taylor?"

"Hee! Yes!" Taylor petted him too. Oh, both of them, and Taylor's boobies still full! More! More!

"Is this something that needs doing often?" Please, Lord, please, except…

"Once in a while, usually special circumstances, but if you aren't willing it would get really awkward." Taylor ran her fingers through the curls at the base of Kenny's neck. "That's why India got rid of that grumpy guy without introductions. Saves time to weed out the grouches and the prudes."

"Miss, I am no prude." And if he was Kenny'd stop the prudery before he offended two pretty women who weren't all the way dressed. He kept his hands and face against Amy's breasts.

"Good, because now we're going to teach you about the pro-milk stimulants." Amy kissed Kenny's hair. "We Dairy Maids need regular applications of prostaglandins to keep up our production, since we don't usually have babies to keep us going."

"Oh." Kenny had no idea what prosta-whatsits were or where to put them. "Okay."

The girls giggled. "Men secrete them."

"They, do?" Kenny hid his bogglement against Amy's tits. If she didn't make him let go, he wouldn't. "Erm, I do? How?"

"Yes, you do." Both girls giggled again, making Kenny's lush handfuls bounce. Holy fuck.

"And to make them work best, you have to apply them to the Dairy Maid's cervix," Taylor informed him, her fingers still working through his hair.

"Cerv..." He had to look up at them, be sure he was hearing what he thought he was hearing. "I don't know how to manage that without..."

"That's why we have to like our hired man quite well, Kenny." Amy smiled again, her teeth bright against her rosy lips and creamy skin. "Because yes, that's exactly what you do."

"Plus it works best if the Dairy Maid climaxes, which means just any old man won't do." Taylor's words sent Kenny into heaven. He'd have to, no, get to bed these women? As part of his job?

"Miss Taylor, are you quite sure I don't have to pay the Dairy?"

*That* got him smacked upside the head. Amy was quite severe, saying, "Don't even joke about that if you want to work here."

He pulled back so they could see his contrition and rub his boxed ear. "Didn't mean to offend, ladies, but it sounds too good to be true."

"Oh, it's true, it's true," Amy said, suddenly losing her ability to say a proper R.

"Maybe it's twu." Taylor developed the same disability and the girls both laughed. "We'd better see."

"So, what have you got?" Amy flicked her fingers at him. "Off with the clothes."

Oh shit, dick size did matter to working here? He thought he had enough, and the motion of the ocean ought to count for something. What was Dirk Manley packing in those tight jeans, and were the Dairy Maids going to compare them? Kenny popped open his pearl-snapped shirt, knowing his chest was broad with muscles gained from hard work.

The girls sucked air through their teeth at the horseshoe-shaped scar below his left nipple. "That's healing. Don't slow me up much," Kenny exaggerated. It wouldn't slow him up at all for what they wanted him to do now. But still his hands went more slowly to his belt buckle.

"Come, on, come on!" Taylor urged, and reached to help him. "Or we'll think you don't like us." Her busy little fingers found the tab on his zipper.

"I like you both right fine." Both, ohmygawd, what was he going to do with two of them? Since they made it clear he needed to cum inside them. Oh holy hallelujah fuck, Amy was lifting her skirt. She hadn't been wearing panties all this time. He'd been kneeling between her knees and closer to heaven than he thought. "What… How?" Because Taylor wasn't lifting her skirt. No, she was taking his jeans down, and the huge lump of his wood was gonna spring out and bat her on the nose. He helped her take his jeans down.

Oh man, if she licked him like that again he'd spray those prostagloppies all over her face!

Taylor wrapped her hand around his cock, pinching hard at the base. "You give Amy a nice big dose of semen, 'kay?"

"Anything you say." Bless her for clarifying what they wanted, for now, maybe he'd get his dick into her too, but one pussy at a time was all he could fuck, and he was being summoned.

"Come here, big boy." Amy had her eyes firmly at his groin. "Think we've had enough foreplay?"

"Yes'm." Fuck, he wasn't even gonna try to get his boots off, his jeans could stay at his knees, because stripping would keep him away from that juicy pink pussy for thirty seconds too long. Oh man was she wet! Her gash opened as she spread her knees to reveal his target, aimed with the light track of her Brazilian. As if he needed help to know where to go, not hardly. All his nursing at her nipples had to be foreplay enough to get her that soppy. Oh damn, perfect, perfect… Kenny hopped to the bed, to bear her down flat to the quilt. She wrapped her legs around his ass, and his heat-seeking missile found the wetness of her channel.

Oh fuck, she was pulling him in, demanding his rampant cock in her wet pussy! Even with all his sucking at her titties, she was tight. But eager. So damned eager.

Kenny thrust his prick into her juicy tunnel, groaning with the pressure of her wet walls.

"How big is he?" Taylor asked from beside them on the bed. Was she gonna watch them? He'd give her something to look forward to.

"Oh, plenty big!" Amy cried. "He's filling me so good!"

He'd fill her all right. He'd stuff her pretty pussy with his thick tool until she blew up into the kind of orgasm that would keep him around to do it again. He pulled out slow, and came back in slow, until she pushed against his ass with her heels. She wanted it faster? He'd give it to her faster, because damn. Just damn.

"Yeah, Kenny, oh that's good. Give it to me, yeah." Amy wrapped every bit of herself, arms legs, pussy, teeth —"Ack!"—she gave off nipping his shoulder, but another six or seven strokes and she could bite him again.

Kissing her might stave off the teeth. Crashing his mouth against hers, he thrust his tongue into her as hard as he thrust his cock into her pussy. Slamming his rigid dick into her, he'd get that semen right where she said she needed it. He just didn't want to spurt too soon, not before she came. He could pull out, eat that delectable pussy a while, but… She wasn't letting go, and her moans got louder with every collision of his cockhead against her cervix.

"Ride me, cowboy," Amy begged, and that was almost enough to make him come, but not yet, she hadn't cried out her own ecstasy, and he'd give her that. Make sure this delicious woman got all the pleasure she was due. For suckling him. For fucking him. For being so damned sweet to him that he was gonna cream in her pussy, just the way she wanted.

Fuck, but those huge titties pressed against his chest. Her nipples made pebbles against his skin, and she was about as pneumatic a girl as ever breathed. He had to bend down to kiss her just to curve over her amazing tits.

Switching to a side to side grind got his groin against her hard little clit. She squeaked and ground back, swiveling those ripe hips under his. She stilled, her head thrown back and her eyes closed. Kenny licked her neck, desperate to help her come, more desperate to get some part of her back in his mouth. She smelled of strawberries and honey and her skin was fine satin under his tongue.

"Keep fucking me, Kenny," she breathed and he didn't need to be told a second time. He'd never been with a girl who wanted it like Amy did. Never jammed his prick into any hole that wanted him like hers did. Never been so glad to give what he wanted the most to someone who wanted it just as bad. Every squeak of the bedsprings was her thrusting up to meet him as much as him pounding down into her.

"Oh, oh!" she cried out, and "Oh!" when he piledrivered into her. "You're fucking me so good!"

"Gotta fuck that sweet pussy," he breathed into her ear. She liked dirty talk? He'd talk dirty. "Gonna fuck it until you come all over my cock. Make you clench and shake and your clit'll throb. You'll squeeze my dick while you come. Squeeze it tight and good, show me how good." With every word he pounded deep between her pussy lips, and she buried her face in his neck.

"Umhh," she squeaked and did exactly what he told her. She shook. She clenched. She held him so tight he could barely breathe, and her thighs held him in place deep inside her. And she throbbed and pulsed around his dick until he couldn't hold it back any more.

He shot his prostawhawhas inside her for what seemed like forever. Draining his nuts into her. Throbbing and pulsing and spurting his cum into her greedy pussy. Blowing up with the kind of pleasure that didn't go with job. He wanted to bring her to a shattering climax, and she'd sure brought him. He throbbed again and a last blob of jizz squirted out of his dick. She'd asked for every drop. And she was smiling when he finally opened his eyes.

"Ahh, Kenny, nice," she breathed when he slid his softening cock out of her. "Real nice."

With a last kiss, he pulled out and lay on his back next to her. What was he supposed to do now? He gave her a shy smile and twined his fingers into hers. Their legs still hung over the edge of the bed, and the covers were rumpled under them. Most comfortable bed he'd ever lain on. Maybe he'd even get to lie all the way on it. If they hired him.

"I hope I've pleased you, Miss Amy," Kenny offered.

"Oh yeah," Amy breathed. "Three times."

"Three!" piped up Taylor. "Wow! And you have a nice ass, Kenny. I wanted to grab your buns so bad!"

Little Miss Unfucked-and-too-chipper had been watching them all this time. Kenny'd managed to forget her.

"That would have been nice," he admitted. Two women wanting him. And him too drained to reach for bouncy-girl, who'd bounced up to bring a wet washcloth.

First she stuffed something into Amy's well-pounded pussy. Squishing a tan disk to fit into her friend's juicy slit, Taylor inserted it between Amy's wet lips and felt around inside her. "Feels like a big healthy dose of prostaglandins. Better wear the diaphragm a while, keep them inside." She withdrew her fingers. Kenny couldn't believe he'd just watched that. Would that be one of his tasks too? Or getting it out?

"Yeah," Amy agreed, and didn't try to cover herself with her skirt. "You give very nice pro-milk stimulation, Kenny." She sighed happily, squeezing her titty to make that well-sucked nipple stand high and shoot a few drops into the air. "I might be filling again already."

If he didn't need a breather so badly, he'd lick the

drops away. Although he was kind of full from her first bounty. And he still had Taylor's titties to suckle. All that milk ought to give a man strength.

Taylor wiped him down, a pleasure in another way. Her cloth was warm and her touch gentle on his hyper-sensitive dick. She cupped his balls delicately and sponged the juices away. She leaned down to place a gentle kiss on his still-shrinking cock. "Your penis is beautiful. I shouldn't have teased you about size."

"We'll see what you say about it after your turn." Kenny found enough energy for a joke, now that he knew they were funning him before. "Um, you do want a turn?"

"Of course I do." Taylor rolled his balls in their sack, her fingertips knowing. "We both have to approve."

Alone in a bedroom with a king sized bed and two bodaciously be-tata'ed beauties had to be the strangest job interview Kenny would ever have, and certainly not one he'd ever expected to have. If this was work in the Manley Dairy, he'd clearly been spending his life on the wrong farms.

## Kenny, Part Two

"FARM WORK, light lifting, high pay for the right applicant" had drawn Kenny into applying for the position, and oh, what a position it was. Right between a beautiful woman's thighs. Applying "pro-milk stimulants." That was stimulating all right, and if the deep drink he'd just taken at Amy's breasts was what he was encouraging, he'd encourage at every opportunity.

Oh man. Here was farm work he could get his back into, even with the nagging horseshoe-shaped injury on his ribs. He'd drive the tractor and mow the hay, whatever, just let him also have duties with Dirk Manley's Dairy Maids. Hot damn. Just hot damn. He'd left his cum inside pretty blonde Amy, and now busty little Taylor was cupping her breasts and mewling anxiously.

"I'm so full!" She jiggled her huge boobies, still

encased in peach lace, though the neckline of her shirt strained below her bust. "I was supposed to take the test for dark blue, too!"

That didn't make a lot of sense to Kenny, though he'd noted that his huge sup of lady-milk had come from a girl wearing a dark blue gingham skirt, now rucked around her waist. Taylor's skirt was a lighter shade.

Amy sat up in a hurry. "Oh! You were! What was India thinking, putting you on interview duty?"

Kenny wanted the Dairy Maids to like him—he had two other job candidates to beat out to stay here on the most marvelous dairy farm in the world. If he got the job, they'd ask his assistance in all the dairy related matters, so if he could bring himself to give up—whatever it was he might have to give up, he'd make the sacrifice.

"Miss Taylor, is there any way you could do both?" Not that he wanted to lose the chance to spray his prosta-thingies into the same wet channel he'd just filled for her companion. But think of the long term—a little easier to do with his dick gone soft.

"Ohh... Yes, but you'd have to be willing to not drink my milk, and I kind of promised..." Taylor gazed at him with long-lashed brown eyes. "But if you don't mind..."

He wanted more—he wanted his lips on those two firm melons she was holding, with the drips soaking the lace at her nipples. But he was real full of Amy's milk. If he got the job, there'd be more of what he'd had so far.

"We already know Kenny's willing to suckle," Amy interrupted. "That's what we really needed to know. And besides, he'd learn more about the dairy if he watched you test."

"Miss Taylor, I'd be pleased to help you do something that sounds this important." *Be helpful, Kenny, then they'll want you to be the hired man here.* That nervous guy and Mr. Shit-eating Grin didn't dare be more agreeable than him! "Isn't this something I ought to know about if I'm going to work here?"

"It's real important to rank in the darkest skirt you can around here." The buxom brunette threw herself into his arms, smushing her enormous, damp titties against his chest. "And yes, you should know, but you'd be giving up my milk. Would you?" She gazed soulfully into his eyes.

"It'll be a real sacrifice," Kenny allowed, "but if you'll explain about ranks and what you're doing, then I'll be content to know I helped." With his arms around her, it was just a little harder to agree.

"Oh, yes!" Taylor pressed her mouth to his and jumped up before Kenny could get any tongue into the kiss. "Let's go down to the demonstration barn and I'll tell you everything on the way!"

Getting dressed meant pulling his shirt down and his jeans up, and the Dairy Maids hid their titties away. Damn. But they each took his hand to guide him downstairs and out the front door. Kenny had the chance to flash a grin at his prospective boss as he was towed by.

"Doing all right there, ladies?" Dirk Manley called after them.

"Wonderful!" Amy yelled over her shoulder. "We like Kenny a lot already!"

Oh, yes, hell to the yes, let him be the one they chose for their hired man. Kenny followed his companions down the hill on a gravel path that curved over a tidy lawn set with croquet wickets. They went past the duck pond, around some outbuildings, past more Dairy Maids with their blouses down and their titties out, suckling men sporting boners and probably smiles.

The women brought him to a white building that didn't look much like a barn, and even less so once they got inside, where an open space was surrounded with three rows of bleachers. Four mysterious pieces of equipment stood in the open arena. "We have events in here, like milk shows and freshenings, and sometimes our guests like to watch us Dairy Maids be milked," Amy explained. "You might have to help with any of those."

Whatever they were. Kenny could hope they involved removing clothing, just as Taylor was doing. She dropped the suspenders of her skirt, shucked out of her white peasant shirt, and let the skirt fall around her ankles. No panties, well, well, well. And that bra was big enough to use for camping. Now that her clasp was undone,

Taylor's huge round titties stood high on her chest, with drips of milk plinking to the wooden floor at her feet.

"Help me, Amy!" she cried. "I can't waste my milk!"

Kenny'd lick it up but instead helped Amy set an aqua basin into one of the racks, which did sort of look like a milking stanchion, now that he thought about the bench and the headrest and the booby-basins. Taylor all but flung herself onto the rack, settling her huge breasts into the basins. Her nipples poked out through the openings at the bottoms. "Hurry, get the milkers on me!"

With a quick look at what Amy was doing, Kenny got his suddenly familiar milker attached to the basin. That would tug and suck away on Taylor's tit. Following the hoses across the floor, Kenny identified the pump. Amy handed him a marked pint bottle to affix to the milker, and then she hit the switch.

The pump began to *whum*, and Taylor smiled. "Oh good. Now help me with the headrest."

Together Kenny and Amy settled the stanchion around Taylor's head, perfect for her to lean her forehead against. Long brunette strands fell against her face, clinging statically to her cheeks. She puffed at her hair. Kenny lifted her hair away from her face, whipping it into a loose braid. Why hadn't she used her hands? Oh.

Her wrists were imprisoned in cuffs. She couldn't lift her hands from the hand rests. But Taylor didn't seem to mind. Nor did she mind bending naked over a padded bench, her ass poking out so deliciously. Her every secret lay exposed to his gaze. Great balls o'fire, this lovely gal shaved her crotch. Her plump lips spread pinkly when she shifted her feet, and her dark pucker peeped from between her round globes of ass. Finally Taylor collapsed with a sigh into the equipment that held her immobile.

"Thanks, guys." She smiled dreamily. "I don't think I lost much."

"You'll make dark blue this time, I just know it." Amy patted Taylor's shoulder. "Light blue is under five ounces a side every six hours," she informed Kenny, "and medium is five to nine ounces. Dark blue means she can give nine ounces or more from each breast every six hours. On average."

Kenny studied the naked woman bent over the milking bench, her breasts spitting their white produce into clear bottles with every pull of the pump. "That's a lot?"

"Oh yes." Amy smoothed her skirt. Dark blue. "Even Lara can't give more than eleven ounces at a time, although she has to pump every four hours. I'm trying to get there..."

"With prostawhatsis and orgasms," he recited, to prove he'd been paying attention to something besides Amy's milky titties and wet pussy back at the house. Kenny'd be delighted to help, and he hoped to meet the bountiful Lara sometime soon. "So Taylor has to prove how much milk she can give?"

"Exactly!" Amy came to hang on his arm. She helped him watch the white jets of milk squirt into the clear collecting bottles. Taylor's dusty rose nipples expanded and contracted in the clear bottle necks. Such perky nubs, and with milk jetting out. He'd never seen anything like it. Tasted it, with Amy, but not seen a woman lactate. Amazing.

"But I still need prostaglandins, Kenny," Taylor said, facing the floor. "To stimulate my milk. You will help, won't you?"

Kenny'd stimulate something all right. Everything was right there for his delectation, and he was invited to delect. "You bet I will."

"Oh good." Taylor smiled dreamily.

"Let's give her a few minutes to get settled, and then…" Amy grinned impishly. "Or do you need a few minutes more?"

"Not now I don't," Kenny declared. His dick had come back to life at the sight of Taylor's plump bottom and sweet, bare pussy. She'd asked him to fuck her, no, she'd begged him to fuck her. A man couldn't stay down in the face of an invitation like that. But a few more minutes wouldn't hurt. He shifted his rising erection inside his underwear. His Johnson hadn't gotten so much action in quite a while, and these two busty ladies were begging for it. Whoo-haw!

Orgasms and prostaglandins, huh. The Manley Dairy hired man would have the best job ever. He'd give this lactating woman the means to keep lactating all she wanted. She wanted semen in her pussy, that meant she wanted his dick bare. Kenny'd stick his prick into her without a condom any day she wanted. Might even put a baby in there, a little calf for the dairy. Better check with Dirk on the policy for that later; he didn't want to spoil this sweet thang's mood. Kenny ran his hand up and down Taylor's back, watching her eyes close dreamily. A soft "Mmm" trickled from her throat.

"You really want me to—do—you while you're getting milked?" He had to ask, but he stumbled over the "fuck" he didn't want to use to her aloud.

"Really do," she sighed, and the pumps pulled away at her nipples.

Amy led him away from the milking rack to a separate room, with a couch and a counter with a sink and drawers. "We need to let her settle into her milking trance, and then you'll take care of her." Amy hugged him hard, or soft and squashy, with those big breasts against his chest. "Just as good as you took care of me."

"I will do my absolute best." Taylor wanted milk. Orgasms and jizz made milk, oh yeah, he could do that.

"Explain what you do with all this milk." Kenny

glanced out at the naked woman in the stanchion, who wasn't moving at all, though her nipples shrank and expanded under the pump's pressure.

Amy giggled. "We have men come from all over the world to drink straight from the source. Plus everything we pump gets shipped out frozen to customers who want the milk or need the nutrition."

"And that's a lot?" Kenny wondered, doing math in his head. Average of eight ounces per breast times two breasts per woman times four milkings a day times how many women? He got a number high enough to make his head hurt.

"About twelve or thirteen thousand ounces a month." Amy pinched her nipple through her blouse. How much of that had she pumped? "And we could ship more if we had it."

"That's where I come in?" Kenny would do his absolute best to make this a productive dairy, starting with the woman he held and the woman being milked.

"Yes, and I think Taylor's ready for you. She looks well into her milking trance." Amy shooed him out the door. "I'll watch your technique from here."

Oh she would? Didn't she have some idea from getting well and truly pounded not an hour ago? But a woman in a bed got different handling than a woman in a stanchion. Kenny'd never heard of a milking trance, but Amy was talking about it like that was desirable, so he wouldn't disturb a good thing. He'd ask questions, but weren't they assessing his good sense along with his enthusiasm for milk and bareback sex?

Sooo… Kenny returned to Taylor's side. *Don't mess with the trance, don't surprise her…* Kenny ran gentle hands along Taylor's back and down her sides. She lay bent against the padded bench, her knees slightly angled and not taking much of her weight. If she got any more relaxed she'd be comatose.

Kenny whispered soft encouragements anyway, nonsense happiness like, "Your skin is so soft, your breasts are giving so much milk. I'm going behind you now, I'm going to give you your prosta…prosta…" Kenny lost the whole word, but got a "Mmm…" that nearly disappeared into the whir and hiss of the pumps.

Orgasms, he was supposed to give her orgasms, but that didn't seem to go with her relaxed state. He knelt behind her and parted her pussy lips with his fingers. She smelled all woman, fragrant with desire and freshness. Never going to get a better chance—he put his mouth to her pussy. Bet he could lick her into contentment, if not a climax, if he ran his tongue along her ridges and down to her clit. *Don't get crazy now, just long smooth strokes, and maybe a little bit of sucking on that stiff nubbin at the end of her slit. Tasty…*

She grew wet with his attentions, a bead of her juices rolling down over her clit. She moaned deep in her throat, and he lapped at her dusky rose core. She seemed to be enjoying herself, even if she wasn't obviously on the brink of any big crashes, but crash + trance= naw, let's keep it soft and easy.

Fine with him—Kenny kept her spread open for his tongue, and ate her out until he'd had his fill. By then her bottles were half full and his cock was completely full, and raring to go again. He rose to his feet and opened his jeans.

Amy'd liked his cock in her pussy just fine. Hope she liked watching her friend get seven fat inches slid into her pussy. Because Kenny worked his dick twice to limber up, and guided the fat cockhead to his milker's juicy puss. Sliding in home, oh, so wet. So good. Warm and juicy—he'd made her real ready, even if she wasn't responding much. Inch by excruciating inch, he pushed into her waiting channel, until his groin pressed against her round buttocks and there was no more "in" to go. The swell of her hips made perfect hand holds. He'd better go slow. Or he'd blow.

He'd given her enough tongue that she might cum, or she might not. Trying to recall what was more important, he decided that jizz and peace were more important than orgasm, though he'd give her that later if she still wanted him to. Right now, just in and out in long lazy strokes. Not disturbing her calm, not getting wild and crazy. Just in and out of the best portal in the world. Kenny watched his dick disappear into her tunnel.

Her dark pucker twitched, like maybe she wanted that touched too, and he'd put a finger in if it didn't risk surprising her. Next time. Goddam, there had to be a next time. But right now was pretty damned good, all deep in her pussy, slow, just out until only the fat knob stayed at her opening and then in until his whole shaft was warm and wet.

She tightened around him, and if this dawdling pace wasn't doing the max for her, it was doing just fine for him. Kenny pulled himself into her puss and stayed while the hell busting loose in his balls filled her cooze with spunk. She wanted spunk, she was getting spunk, and Kenny never had a better time giving a gal what she wanted.

Was like his cream went right through her pussy and out her nipples, 'cause her bottles were damned near full and she was still spraying the white stuff. He leaned over her back with murmured words of praise. "You're milking like a champ, li'l darlin'. Just fillin' up those bottles. You're doing good, and your pussy is heaven."

He'd have said more, but talking to someone who wasn't talking back, just lying there under him weirded him a little, but not enough to make him pull his dick out. He planted a kiss on her shoulder blade and stayed put until his cock softened enough to slide out. Careful not to disturb her, he straightened and pulled up his jeans.

Amy came to see, kneeling to assess her pal's squirts of milk. "Good job, Tay-tay!" but not too loud. To Kenny she said, "We're gonna put this diaphragm in to keep your semen inside her. The longer it stays, the better." She helped him guide a flexible disc into the pussy he'd just finished fucking. "She's over nine ounces and she's just about done. Let's turn off the pumps. She'll start talking to us in a minute."

The pump went quiet. Taylor *hmmf*ed a little, but picked her head up when Kenny started stroking her shoulder just like Amy was. "How'd I do?"

Amy kissed her pal's forehead. "You did beautiful. Almost ten ounces each side!"

"You gave a lot of milk," Kenny added, wanting to see how her breasts looked without huge amounts of milk swelling them. Also, he needed to know— "Did I do you right?"

"Oh, yes." The brunette held her head up so she could be released from the stanchion and the cuffs. Kenny helped her stand, letting her cling. Yup, still pneumatic as all get out, though her breasts had lost the shiny look and were softer when he cuddled her. "You did me perfect. You didn't get fast and bouncy. I stayed in my milking trance."

"That helps production," Amy added, trying to guide one of Taylor's arms through a bra strap.

"Yeah. Did Amy tell you to do that?" Taylor needed three tries to cover one breast with a bra cup, and didn't protest when Kenny finally took over.

Only the dream of being able to release those glorious bazzooms again let Kenny fasten the clasp at her breastbone. "No, but I thought that was important, to not jostle you alert. If you need to cum, I could help you now that you're—awake." He didn't know how else to put it.

"That's sweet of you." Taylor stifled a yawn against the back of her hand. "Maybe after I take a proper nap."

Kenny half-carried, half guided the drowsy Taylor where Amy directed, and together they lay her down on a queen-sized bed in a dorm full of dairy maids. Kenny smiled widely at them, sending "Howdy, miss" out like confetti with telepathic thoughts of *I'm your new hired man, I'm your new hired man.* What would his interviewers tell Dirk Manley?

Amy introduced him to three more Dairy Maids: Rita, Mindy, and Luz. He'd tap any one of them in the name of milk, and now that he knew the code of the skirts, he could interpret Rita's hungry look as "Get me out of this light blue even if you have to fuck me."

One like that in every herd, he supposed.

He didn't miss the protective way Amy sheltered Taylor's milk bottles, like Rita might lunge to take them for her own. "Come on, Kenny, the sooner we get Taylor's milk checked in at the milk house, the better." She all but ran to the door.

Outside again, Kenny dared ask Amy, "Do you think you'll both give me a good recommendation with the boss?"

"Oh, yes!" Amy smiled at him, and her cheeks went pink. "But we still have to find out what the other Dairy Maids decide about Brett and Travis."

Would they end up with the nervous kid or the knowing man instead of him? No, no, no. Kenny stopped to lift Amy's chin to look her full in the eye. "Miss Amy, I can drive a tractor and plow a field just as good as I can take care of a lady in bed. I have never wanted a job so much in my life."

## Brett

WHEN HE APPLIED at the Manley Dairy, Brett didn't think there'd be much competition for the job. Most folks liked more nightlife and less hard work. So why was he one of three, oops, now four men waiting in the farmhouse parlor for the Dairy Maids? One guy couldn't stop grinning, one looked a little nervous, and one man looked like he had some serious corncob where the sun didn't shine.

How was he supposed to make a good impression on a bunch of women? Brett hadn't had any particular success talking to women in general, and he hadn't had much exposure to any over high school age. Heck, he wouldn't be sitting here if his folks hadn't insisted that he go learn other folks' farming methods before taking over at the family spread.

He knew about cows, not women, and he wasn't getting any insight at all from this magazine he was trying to read upside down. He was gonna get all tongue tied, he just knew it, and he'd probably offend them by staring at their tits, and then he'd say something stupid like, "Lovely breasts you have there, Miss."

Just because he didn't have much experience with women didn't mean Brett didn't want some. Too many nights alone with some Bag Balm and his right hand, no girlfriend, and no way to get a girlfriend left him plenty of time to fantasize. He hadn't grown out of his gangly phase until he'd gotten out of high school, and the three years since graduation had been spent with more cows than people. The girls who hadn't looked at him twice back then would look at him now that he topped six feet and had some shoulders. His jeans still fell off without a belt—why the heck couldn't he find britches both long enough and skinny enough?

He'd hit the barbershop in Pennington before coming out for his interview, so at least his brown hair looked good and his chin was fresh-shaven, and maybe the Dairy Maids would give him points for smelling good. Or would they think he was a dandy and not willing to work?

Oh dear sweet—fuck. Here they came. Dirk Manley called out the front door for the Dairy Maids, and now the parlor was full to bursting with beautiful women in white blouses and blue skirts. Tall ones, short ones, blondes, brunettes, a redhead. A tall black woman with a thousand tiny braids and a smile fit to blind him. Heck, every one of these women was smiling. At him.

Brett's dick stood up to greet them about as fast as he did. That much blood rushing south left him lightheaded. The magazine might hide his chubby but not his confusion. He missed names and everything the women said turned into so much garble. He was staring. He knew he was staring and he couldn't help it. These gals were well-endowed. What was bigger than well-endowed? Their huge breasts made a band of clear focus, everything above and below their bosoms fuzzed out of existence. Huge. Breasts. On a dairy. Big, big breasts.

Brett's brain shorted out completely. He mumbled something to their greetings. The corncob fellow got sent upstairs—upstairs?!—with two of the women, and that didn't leave any more air in here than there'd been.

He had to talk to these women. And the only head he could think with was his little one, which wasn't real little now. Nope, hard, throbbing, and couldn't be relied on for words.

His brain came back enough to register when the tall black woman spoke his name. "Chelle, Emily, you take Brett here."

*Chelle, Emily, Chelle, Emily* he repeated silently, and lost the names completely when Corncob came pounding downstairs again, shouting "These women are crazy!" And then he was gone, roaring away in his truck.

Less competition, but—crazy? Brett didn't care about their sanity. When he couldn't say a coherent word, how would that matter?

The tall black woman, who sounded like the boss, *hmphed.* "Didn't think he'd last long anyway." She slid her arm into the crook of one of the other men, the confident one. "Kitty and I will assess ol' Travis's suitability for the Dairy, down by the hickory grove."

"We'll show Brett the barn," said one of the blondes. She took his arm and smiled up at him.

Barns were at least familiar territory. Brett stumbled out of the farmhouse with one lovely, busty woman on each arm, and not a single word could he form. Dirk flashed him a grin and a wish for luck.

He'd need it, because creaming his jeans on the way to the barn was a real possibility.

The women clutched him and steered him, chatting at and around him. "I'm Chelle," said the woman in the brown braids. He'd have to remember that, because she and Emily were dressed the same in blue gingham skirts and white blouses. The suspenders on their skirts made their titties stick out so far...

That left the blonde in the pony tail to be Emily, and she wanted to point out the sights of the farm, like Dr. Busby's clinic (huh?) and the duck pond.

"We're here!" Emily announced, and headed up the ladder.

"With horses?" Brett thought he'd be quizzed on cows. But if he could look up her skirt, he'd talk horses.

"Yes!" Chelle exclaimed happily. "Horses smell better and this loft's quiet." She pushed him at the ladder. "Go on up!"

He followed Emily up the ladder—was she wearing pink panties?—one dogged step at a time. Up top, he let her lead him behind a big drift of loose hay, into a secluded area where the light came in through the slats and a big green blanket lay spread over the hay. Emily plopped down on the blanket, patting the spot next to her. "Let's talk about milk!"

"Erm, what about milk?" Brett could talk butterfat and pounds per cow, but she had her hands under those huge titties, lifting them like an offering. Words fled again.

"Our milk!" Chelle said, like that was entirely obvious. The way she pinched at a damp spot on her breast, maybe it was.

"Your—" He'd suspected, maybe hoped, but she was saying he was right? "I don't—" He did but he didn't believe it.

"Yes!" Both women pulled their blouses down, exposing their ginormous boobies.

Brett stared—he'd never met tits dressed only in bras, especially not lacy bras. "Your—"

"Well yes, of course." Chelle opened a clasp between her breasts. The cups eased apart and she shrugged them away. Her breasts were free, uncovered, and—was that a white drop on her nipple?

"Oh dear, I don't think Dirk explained very well!" Emily chirped. "We're Dairy Maids, we provide the milk, and our new hired man has to help with milking and with applying pro-milk stimulants."

"Yeah…" Bret's head swam—four bare breasts, four enormous bare breasts filled his vision. Enormous, bare, drippy breasts… Four of 'em.

"Aw, Brett," Emily cooed. "You're acting like you've never seen breasts before."

"I haven't," he choked out. "Not for real."

"Really?" Chelle perked up, shooting quizzical glances at Emily and back to Brett. "You mean…?"

"I think he does, Chelle." Emily scooted closer and slipped her hand into his.

"I don't have much experience with the ladies," Brett admitted through the flames consuming his face. His cheeks might set the hay on fire. "Erm, not any."

"None at all?" Chelle marveled.

"Nope. Sorry." Maybe he should leave, head out and pretend he'd never heard of the Manley Dairy.

"Oh, Emily! We've found a virgin!" Chelle squealed out the terrible word. She clutched his arm so tightly he couldn't run, not with her leaking titties pressed against him like that. Not with Emily's dripping nipples dampening his sleeve.

He didn't want to admit the truth to his captors. He wanted to run, pretend he'd never heard them say that horrible word. His dick wanted to stick around to find out what they'd do about it.

Brett's cock was the hardest it had ever been in his whole life, and the closest to a woman it had ever been. His arms were happy, but his dick wanted in on all the grabbing. Chelle and Emily rubbed their breasts against him even harder, and Chelle kissed his cheek.

"Aw!" Brett didn't say shucks, but his dick said hell to the yes! And he came. Filled his chonies. Brett grabbed his traitor crotch, while the fireworks blew in his balls and shot out his cock.

"Oh, dear, did you just come?" Emily frowned at his dampening crotch. "That's wasteful. We need the prostaglandins in your semen."

"Sorry," he gasped. Why was she worried about where he'd shot off and not *that* he'd shot off? "I'll try not to do it again." Fuck, had he really just done that?

"Good. We need you to put them in our vaginas."

Brett quit breathing. He knew only one way to get what they wanted where they wanted. And no experience in doing it. "You...do.... Uh... okay."

"Erm, your virginity's not religious, is it? Emily asked. Brett shook his head. He didn't even have that excuse.

"We need the prostaglandins," Chelle pondered. "You'd be willing to have us devirginize you?"

Would he be willing to let them make his every fantasy come true? Two beautiful girls with big bare breasts and the promise of pussy? Time to man up and take what they were offering. "Ladies, you can do whatever you want with me."

"Ooh, yes!" they squealed. "We'll take good care of you!" promised Chelle.

"Milk first," decreed Emily, pushing him flat to the blanket on the hay. They loomed over him, their breasts huge. Four stiff nipples, all letting drops fall on his face. "Brett, our hired man has to suckle milk sometimes. Will you try?"

Oh yeah! He opened his mouth, and Emily leaned down. She put her nipple right in his unbelieving mouth. Her nipple! They were going straight to sucking!

Oh, my goodness, creamy milk gushed from her with every suck. Her milk, Oh jeez! Oh man! Brett hardly knew what to do, but his mouth had the idea. He flicked his tongue across the nubbin of his dreams. He had to swallow, and swallow again, just to keep up with her flow.

"Yes, you're doing a good job, Brett!" Emily placed his hand on her free breast. "Suck me dry." Her huge tit was so firm, with swollen bumps under the fine skin. He'd be hard again in no time at all!

Chelle found something to do. Hands worked at his belt, his zipper came down, and she tugged. Wouldn't take much effort to pants him. He lifted his hips and a woman made him naked in her sight.

"Oh, Emmy! He has such a pretty cock!"

He did?

"At least seven inches and so fat!" She wrapped both hands around his shaft.

No woman had ever admired his equipment. No woman had ever handled his cock. He'd never had dainty hands gripping his dick before, never felt the whisper of breath against his head. Never felt—oh lord—was that her tongue? Oh hell yeah!

His first cum might have been a good thing—he could last more than twenty seconds with her lips on his dick. He suckled harder, getting more and more milk to spray from Emily's nipple. He was gonna drown in this much milk, he was gonna go out happy…With a mouth full of titty and a hand full of titty and his dick in a woman's mouth. Heaven couldn't be any better than this.

And then Emily took his treasure away, popped her nipple right out of his mouth. "Good job, Brett." She leaned down to kiss him, her mouth as warm and her tongue as mobile as her pal's. He hugged her with one arm and reached down to the marvel giving him head.

Her hair was soft and smooth, tumbling down from the ponytail over his hand.

"Is this nice?" Chelle had to release his cock to ask. *Please more sucking, please no talking...*

"'Mazing," he gurgled. "I think... I might cum again real soon, the way you're doing that."

"Lovely, but first..." She squeezed the base of his dick and the orgasm backed down. Was she really pulling up her skirt?

Oh yes she was! And that was her pussy, open and wet in its nest of blonde curls. Brett had never even had his hand in a girl's panties and now a girl with no panties was swinging aboard.

"Hey, how do you rate going first?" Emily demanded.

His first time and he had girls fighting over giving it to him!

"You gave him first tit," Chelle pointed out. "And you're going to give him second tit while I ride this bronco."

"Your milk is so delicious I want some more, please." Brett wanted everything to keep happening! "Or don't I get both sides?"

"Yes, you do," Emily returned to business. She tickled her nipple, making it hard and crinkly.

And Chelle pointed his cock straight up and touched the fat head to her wet pussy. Oh jeez. Oh jeez. He had to remember this forever, the way she slid down his pole.

Oh she was tight, and hot, and wet. Everything he'd dreamed of only better, and she wanted his cock in her pussy.

She settled on his groin, with his dick filling her up, and she stayed, smiling down on him with her big boobies poking out and the milk falling in droplets onto his belly. He'd never seen anything that beautiful, until Emily leaned down and all he could see was her breast.

Brett wanted to be two men, one to fuck Chelle with his full attention and one to suck on Emily with his full attention. He had both. Oh man, he had both, and if sucking on the girls' titties made them feel half as good as having his prick in Chelle's pussy, he'd have to suck them dry three times a day. Four. He'd do anything to keep Chelle rising and falling on his stiff dick. He didn't think anything could feel better than his rod in her mouth, until he put his rod in her pussy.

She fucked him slow—oh hell, she could fuck him any way she liked. She knew what she was doing, and it didn't matter if he didn't—she was driving, and she was driving him to paradise, one cock-length at a time.

Strokes and suckles, strokes and suckles, oh yeah. Oh. Just…oh…

Emily's milk filled his mouth with gush after gush. He held her breast, massaging ever greater streams out. Her sweet cream flooded his tongue.

His salty cream flooded Chelle's pussy. The lightning

and the thunder pulsed in his gland and his balls and shot out his dick. She milked him, squeezing his cum out with strong clenching. Damn! Just damn. He'd been missing this, all these years, but now he got the man's portion with a vengeance, with convulsions and throbbing and streams of milk in his mouth.

Emily took her nipple away—he'd been down to small mouthfuls before he shot off. Chelle stilled, sitting full down on his rod. Keeping him inside, like she needed him in there.

"Uh, Chelle, did you cum?" He had no way of knowing, lost as he was in his own explosions.

"No, and I should, really." She made a sideways thinky-face. "Orgasms encourage our milk. I got your semen, but we really should be sure I get all the stimulation you can give me."

"And I need some prostaglandins too!" Emily blurted. "It's all part of your interview!"

Yeah! Now that he'd found the way to plowing heaven's little acre, he had another field. "I'd be glad to give you whatever you like, Emily. Anything to keep that delicious milk coming."

Oh man, he still had one beautiful woman on his dick and another was wailing for her turn.

"You still have to suckle me!" Chelle lifted her titties, round and bouncy. Her nipples stood up in rosy peaks, with white droplets growing and falling away. His belly was wet with her dribbles, almost as wet as his cock with her juices.

"Be glad to." Brett sat up, careful not to dislodge Chelle, but he wanted to hug her and kiss her just a little. For showing him what a man should know, and for wanting him in spite of not having pretty words to court her with. He had an arm for Emily, too, and she hugged on him with those big bare titties, the titties he'd drained the way Chelle drained his nuts. "I'm going to need a couple minutes, though."

Maybe not more than one or two. Maybe three at the most. Because Chelle didn't want to get off his cock—she wanted to put her titty into his mouth where she sat.

Fine with him. Brett put his mouth to her rosy target and suckled that milk dispenser like he knew what he was doing. And maybe he did—he'd drained Emily's breasts and made her smile, made her like him enough to fight for the right to fuck him first. Oh, these lovely gals would get all the fucking they wanted. And there was a whole Dairy of them!

He drank. He suckled Chelle's nipple and swallowed her milk, warm from the lady and as delicious as her friend's. He could suck on her titty all day, at least until it was time to put his dick in again, and if they were acrobatic, he wouldn't have to let go while he did it.

"You're hogging him!" Emily complained, her tits bouncing with her indignation. "Brett!"

"He's mine until I'm empty, girlfriend." Chelle had her arms around Brett's shoulders and her nipple in his mouth. "You can wait your turn." She giggled and flexed down below. Brett inhaled a mouthful of milk.

Emily thumped his back right vigorously, and Brett finally caught his breath. "I think I'm okay now." He sought after her breast before mentioning that he might need another two minutes to come up again, but his Johnson would start nosing at her wet folds again, she'd know how his horny-meter was doing.

But damn, did he enjoy the way Emily curled around behind him, her tits pressed to his back. They were softer for not being stretched with milk, but warm, and her nipples stayed up, making pebbles against his skin. She leaned on him, and Chelle fed him, and his dick couldn't stay down.

"Am I about dry there, sweetie?" Chelle combed her fingers through his hair.

"Yes, and you were delicious." He released her nipple with a sigh and a kiss. "You were both delicious. Mmm, thanks."

"We know he's happy to suckle, and he gives really nice prostaglandins." Chelle kissed his cheek.

"I wouldn't know!" Emily grumbled. "I need some."

He'd never have a better chance to ask. "Ladies, before I go giving prosty—things, could I—?" Once the question started, he couldn't finish it. But they knew he'd never done this, so maybe they'd take mercy?

"What would you like, Brett?" Emily kissed the edge of his ear. "Would you like to touch? Or look?"

"Or compare?" Chelle added saucily.

He froze. Would it be as easy as saying yes? "I would. Um, all of that."

Both girls laughed. "Well certainly!" trilled Chelle, and "Let's make it easy, and keep you from losing all your prostaglandins there," from Emily.

A man could die of blushing when the girl he'd just fucked for the first time ever and the girl who wanted to be fucked right now both went and lay down on the blanket, side by side. They both had their skirts rucked up around their waists, and panties, hah. None. Four wondrous tits poked upwards all in a row. Whoa.

"Open your legs, Chelle," nagged Emily, and spread her thighs wide. "Let Brett look."

"Beautiful," was all he could breath, with moist pussy lips spread for him to see. Chelle gaped a little and white dribbles escaped. He'd filled her with that? Yeehaw, he had. He grinned, because right next to pounded pussy was to-be-pounded pussy, all rosy pink and stiff. Was that her clit?

Must be. Two clits, like teensy dicks, and stroking dick was the best feeling he'd ever had until just now.

"You can touch, Brett," Emily suggested.

"One hand for each of us." Chelle winked.

"Two hands for me, since she just got fucked," pouted Emily, and then she went *Oof* when her pal elbowed her.

"Let's keep it fair," Brett allowed. "Because I am going to… to…" Oh how could he say that to a girl? Even if he was going to do exactly that.

"To fuck me," Emily supplied, ever so helpfully. "Put your finger in. That feels nice."

And oh man, he did. One hand for each of them, sliding that long middle finger in and out and in and out. So slow. Girls felt like that inside? Little folds and tiny bumps, all wet and slippery? Except some of that was his, he'd gone and filled Chelle with his spunk. Just like she wanted.

Both of his beautiful interviewers went slack with what he was doing, and he dared to add some thumb. Roll those clitties around, press a little here and a little there. Explore. Tickle some this and some that and find out how deep those damp tunnels went back. Oh nice. Brett's own face went a little slack. "Does that feel good?"

"Oh yes!" Chelle breathed. "A little faster, right, up, right…. oh there!"

One girl for each hand and they were moaning and making noises and quivering, just like he might know what he was doing. He'd put his face down to lick, maybe… But then he couldn't see them, and the one he wasn't licking would complain, and there'd be time.

They'd hire him so they could teach him the fine points of doing them. He wanted more milk, or he would, and now he was ready for some more juice. More pussy juice.

His dick stood up straight again, straight as it ever did with that little curve up toward his belly. Ready to plunge into the slippery channel where he had two fingers in each girl, they could take it, and Chelle had taken his fat cock, she'd said it was pretty, and Emily wanted his dick in her pussy, or why else would she be sitting up to tug him down on top of her?

Chelle whimpered and clapped her own hands to her crotch. He needed two hands for the gal he was going to fuck, and Chelle seemed to know what she wanted—she rolled to her side to watch him slide that big boy right into her friend's pussy.

Old Johnson went inside like he was born to go into pussies, well he was, and he did. Brett couldn't find enough air now that he lay on top of Emily and her giant titties, and his dick went in, in, in until it had to come back out.

Hot damn, he had this lovely gal stretched out in the hay while he made sure the last of his virginity got pumped into nothingness. Chelle rode him, and now he had Emily flat on her back, her bare tits squashed against his chest. With every thrust of his hips he shoved his prick deep into her mysterious chasm. Brett could explore in there all night and all day and never know every contour.

Emily yipped with the pounding he was giving her. Smacking his cockhead against the end of her channel felt so damn good, and those weren't "stop, do something else" noises coming out of Emily. No siree they were not —she panted and set her teeth into his shoulder. Spreading her legs for him wasn't enough, not for this darling gal, no, she had to wrap her legs around his ass and urge him on with a dainty foot jammed into his crack. So she had some opinions on the speed and the depth? Great, cause he'd waited long enough in his life to give a woman a good, long fuck.

The hay crinkled under his elbows, where the blanket scratched at his forearms. The loft rang with his panting and hers, and the dim cool was heated with Chelle's arm over his back and her hot breath mingling with theirs. Brett's hips snapped their primal rhythm, even when Emily clenched him, with arms, legs, lips, and muff.

She cried out under his thrusting, quivering with the pleasure he'd fucked her into. Damn, just damn, and then everything south of his navel went to molten lava, pulsing and throbbing from deep inside and out his cock.

If he didn't pour as much spunk into her as he'd left elsewhere, he still put it where it would do her the most good. Thin ribbons splattered the very end of her tunnel, and whatever the hell it was in his jizz that she wanted, she got. As much as he had left, it was all hers. Yay for being twenty-two and studly, he had enough of what two women wanted to give a share to each.

Long minutes passed while they caught their breaths. Brett gently disentangled himself from his partner and rolled into the gap Chelle created. He snuggled one girl into each armpit, their heads on his shoulders, and their tits above and below him like pontoons. Tits so big they needed to be treated like personages, and some lunatic joke bubbled in the back of his mind that perhaps he should give those breasts their own names. Chelle-Marie and Chelle-Paulette maybe, and Emily-Anna and Emily-Jean. So wonderful to be hugged up with these gals. All six of 'em.

"Did I make you happy?" he dared to ask, once he thought he knew the answer.

"Oh yes," said one and "You did," confirmed the other, sweet murmurs against his chest.

"Enough to keep me on around here?" What else could he have done? Licked them? Would he get a chance to try?

"Oh, I think so." Chelle squeezed him. "Lots of native talent and no bad habits to break."

"Darlin', any on the job training you give me will be more than welcome, 'cause I don't want no bad work habits." Brett dared to kiss the tops of their heads, and hoped the other two men had nothing but bad habits. "I will be the hardest worker you ever did have on this dairy."

Chelle gripped his cock, soft now and a little sticky, and gave it a squeeze. It jumped in her hand. She giggled. "Not at the moment, but overall—yes, you just might be."

Travis

_______

MAYBE ALL THOSE tall tales Uncle Horace told about his job weren't such lies after all. Travis sat through his interview with the owner of the Manley Dairy, listening between the words and hearing the echoes of his uncle. Beautiful women who needed su—well, maybe he should keep to business for a little while longer. Or his grin might split his face a little too soon and Dirk Manley would think Travis's enthusiasm was a bit misplaced.

Nope, didn't want much more from Dirk Manley than a firm handshake and "You start Monday at 5 a.m. Milk the cows first."

Because Uncle Horace's stories had been pretty sweet. Being hired man around here sounded eighty-leven times better than working any other farm with any other crop.

Sure, there were fields and livestock and chores, but there were Dairy Maids.

How many of them now? Sixteen? Eighteen? Travis couldn't keep the names straight, although a few stuck out in his memory for Uncle Horace's stories. That Heidi, mentioning her put a glint in Horace's eye, and his tales of Luz, well, Travis knew how to be a gentleman and he wouldn't be getting on her bad side. Rita now, she ought to be good for a lot of what Travis wanted, if she was so desperate… And India—Travis didn't think any woman, no matter how fat and sassy, could get the better of him. Of course, he didn't think his uncle was an easy one to get the better of either, but maybe the old man was getting soft.

Heh, the softer his uncle got, the more "chores" Travis expected to take on around here. The kind of chores that only a hired man who "got along very well" with the Dairy Maids, as his prospective boss had put it, could do.

Oh yeah, Travis was ready to be real friendly.

Not to the three other men now sitting in the parlor, waiting for the second part of their interviews. One was barely more than a kid, and he had to be worried he couldn't measure up to a real man, the way that magazine rattled in his hand. Not that he could read a word of it upside down. Travis didn't think Kid was any kind of competition. Probably terrified of women.

The man with the ramrod straight back and the

grouchy face looked like a shoo-in for first reject. Bet he only did his wife on Saturday nights, missionary position, and after three hours of penitential prayer. No competition there—Reverend Ramrod would eliminate himself just as soon as he got whiff of the Dairy Maids.

Two down, and one other real contender. The last one to come in, good-looking and calm. That guy could be a problem. Time to cast a little doubt. Travis grinned at him, with a big dollop of "I know something you don't know" in it, and watched the guy swallow. *Yeah, buddy, get your guts twisted so you do something dumb and leave me as the only real choice for this plum job.*

And now Dirk Manley was calling out the door. "Come in, my dear Dairy Maids!"

Oh buddy, look at all this dazzling lady-flesh! Tall, short, plump, thin, blonde, brunette, redhead, black, one of everything. Except little tits. Not a one of them that didn't have tatas out to here. All dressed in white blouses and blue skirts with suspenders. Bless Uncle Horace for his hints and directions and winks, 'cause Travis wasn't about to make an ass out of himself for staring, though they all looked good enough to stare at.

Big, black, and sassy had to be India, couldn't be two of 'em, could there? She started directing traffic, sending the Reverend Corncob upstairs with, huh, so that was Rita, and the busty redhead.

Only then did she give names. "I'm India, here's Chelle, Kitty, Emily, Amy, and Taylor."

Oh, good, he was right. Travis smiled his best at her, 'cause if India didn't like him, he was toast. Or so said Uncle Horace.

"Chelle and Emily, you take Brett here. Taylor, Amy, you get Kenny, and Travis, you come with me and Kitty. Think we can all get along?"

Oh hell yes. Especially if their idea of getting along involved taking off those white blouses and lifting blue skirts.

Footsteps thudded down the staircase.

The Rev paused at the front door long enough to yell, "These women are fucking crazy! I'm out of here!" The door slammed behind him, and a pickup truck's roar followed.

The guy would enjoy himself more if he switched to a livelier denomination, maybe the Church of the Open Bottle. Travis wasn't sorry to see him go.

One of the blondes *tsk'd.* "We really shouldn't let Rita interview."

The two women came downstairs more slowly, and the redhead waved on their way out the door.

India *hmphed.* "Didn't think he'd last long anyway." Taking Travis's arm, she said, "Kitty and I will assess ol' Travis's suitability for the Dairy, down by the hickory grove."

Bring on the hickory grove! He watched pairs of lovelies escort his competition out. He'd bet his next year's worth of paychecks at this job or any that they couldn't duplicate what he was about to show his pair of Dairy Maids. Hardly a matched set, one tall and dark and the other petite and brunette. Travis's pecker eyed them blindly and pronounced them perfect.

Travis winked at Dirk Manley on his way out the door. Oh yeah, he'd be working here.

His interviewers led him across a wide lawn studded with croquet wickets and past a duck pond. Fields rolled out in the distance and a faint whiff of cow made him think of his uncle, who did heavy work with the stock and still had some time for chores with the Dairy's main attractions. Travis licked his lips.

"We gonna have a respect problem, you and me?" India's grip on his arm grew dangerously tight.

"Don't think so," Travis replied easily. "You and Uncle Horace get along okay, don't you?" He looked her straight in the eye, more than a match for her six-foot tall frame. A couple hundred thin braids swung dangerously behind her, clicking their beads on her ass. He wanted to get his hands into that mass of hair, preferably from behind.

"He's your uncle, huh," she snorted. "Then maybe you already got the idea that I run the Dairy Maids. No job title, but I don't need no stinking job title."

"Don't imagine you do." He'd noticed Dirk stepping out of her way.

"And don't think you know everything about the Dairy already, just 'cause you have relations working here," she warned him. "We still surprise the old timers."

"You're surprising me all right." Travis flexed his fingers, gone a little numb under her grip. "I'd think you'd want your hired men to have full use of both hands."

"Hah!" India barked, but she let go all the same. Kitty, silent on his other side, giggled lightly.

They passed a Dairy Maid and a man in dude clothes, pressed creases in his jeans and all, heading the other way on the path following the creek. She nodded at India. "The grove's empty."

"Good, good."

"Why?" Travis asked. He'd let them educate him.

"Because then no one can hear you scream," Kitty murmured.

What? Travis stopped short and stared at the butter-wrapper vision who'd just sprouted fangs and a devil's tail. "You're joking."

She thrust out her huge breasts and her lower lip. "You heard that man say he thinks we're crazy. But we're not, and we don't like when people yell that in front of our guests. Most of them understand, but it's still not nice."

"Besides, if this interview goes well, the only screaming is the good kind." India slapped his ass. "Keep going. Or don't. It'll make our decision easy."

"I'm going, I'm going!" Travis picked up the pace and dragged his companions along the path. "Where are we going?"

"This is good," India declared when they'd reached a small meadow with a pond, ringed with tall hickory trees. "Quiet, and that tree's not too ridgy to lean on."

"It's pretty." He glanced around. Good to keep in mind for any extracurricular activities once he'd gotten the job.

India put both hands on her hips. "So, tell us what you think you know about the Dairy Maids and the hired man's duties."

Oh no, he wasn't going to tell her Horace's more pungent stories, especially not the ones that featured her. "Every one of you lactates. Sometimes you need help milking. Help getting milked."

She nodded, her full dark lips spreading in a smile. "That's right. How do you think you do that?"

Ah, this Travis knew from his uncle's stories and a hundred nights of imagination. "You have pumps, but sometimes you need a man's mouth on your tits."

"He doesn't mince words, India." Kitty nodded approvingly. "That's good." Her dark curls bounced against her breasts.

"Ah, yeah. And what else?" India didn't relax much.

"That you need semen, or some substance in it, to keep lactating." Travis didn't think he could repeat the chemical's name accurately, so he didn't try. He picked his next words carefully. "And some of you don't mind if you get the semen the usual way."

There, not as crude as "You need to be fucked until your eyes cross."

India threw her head back and laughed. "I'd say you got the basics. Now—" She pulled her blouse down. She unsnapped something and her deep blue bra cups parted. "You think you're enough of a man to start milking?"

"Hell yes I am." Travis stared at her breasts. Huge, round, full. The skin stretched tight across their width, and her nipples dark to near purple standing stiff on equally dark targets. Damn, but she was big, and full! White droplets grew on the tips and plinked away into the grass. "Tell me how you'd like it."

"Well, well, we have a real go-getter here." India motioned to a couple of fallen logs, one lower than the other. "Sit down right here, and get a big mouthful."

Travis sat down between her thighs, and wrapped both hands around one of India's breasts. He'd never known how good his tan would look against such dark lushness. He licked his lips and then her nipple. And started to suck.

"Yow!" India smacked his shoulder. "I said a big mouthful!"

Travis blinked. "I did."

"Of my tit, dumbass, not the milk. Get a good big mouthful and squeeze from down here." She demonstrated, pinching at the very edge of her areola. Travis wiped the stream of milk off his face. "—not just the tip. That hurts, and if you hurt me twice, you're done."

"Sorry." Boy was he. He didn't want to be done, so he followed instructions, even though she was making a big deal out of nothing. He sucked on women's tits all the time, just not with milk. But if she wanted him to do it a certain way, okay. For now.

Damn, but his uncle hadn't said one tenth of how good it was to suck. Once he got the hang of it, and got used to the taste. Like nothing he'd ever put in his coffee for sure, but damn. Ladymilk! Travis suckled and swallowed, and resisted pulling off to spray his face with her tit. He wanted to see the white fluid fly out, see where it came from and how. He tried with his tongue, finding streams and sprays, nothing he could feel as finely as he wanted to know. Damn she had a lot of milk! He kept drinking, and her tit softened under his hands.

Never sucked on a lady of such deep complexion. She was lovely at close range, and her milk was slightly sweet and getting creamier with each swallow. She smiled down at him, and offered a second breast when she decided he'd finished her first one. He'd gotten so much already, but he was thirsty for anything that put her tit in his mouth. One of four he planned to suckle. What else could he do with these gals? Was everything else his uncle hinted at true as well? 'Cause her skirt was slipping up her thighs.

Orgasms, Horace had said. Orgasms spurred their production. Hope the old man wasn't funning him on that. Because India's skirt had crept up damn near to her crotch and Travis wasn't sure she was wearing any panties.

Time to find out. Without letting go. He slipped his hand between her thighs. India chuckled deep in her throat and eased her legs apart.

"Oh yes, we have a go-getter, Kitty." India patted the log beside her. "Better come see what he's doing in case, ah, I lose track."

He'd make her lose track all right. Course, he might fall off this here log first, because she wasn't wearing any panties. Where he thought he'd find a cotton barrier, or maybe satin, he found bare skin. Not a hair on this pussy, and he was stroking away. Wanted her to change her mind now if she was going to, because once he got started, he didn't want to stop. Not when he had juicy pussy under his fingertips. He must be doing something right—she was wet.

Real wet—so slick his fingers skated right over her private folds. In was an inch away, but he'd diddle her until she smiled on him. Like she was doing now. Guess she liked little circles around her clit.

"Think you're gonna start on the cumming early huh," she teased him, but she didn't sound like she minded, not with both hands on his shoulders and her knees far apart.

"Uh huh," Travis grunted around her titty, and eased his finger in. He needed the other hand to ease his dick, can't have that getting bent, the way it was trapped in his clothes. He wanted his jeans gone, the better to point his rod at her lush pussy, just the minute she seemed receptive. She seemed to like his fingers well enough—she spread her thighs and let him ease a second finger in.

"He's doing pretty good, huh, India?" whispered Kitty. She sat on the fallen log next to India, clutching her pal's arm, just cute as a button next to big and elegant.

"Right fine, honey." India cupped a hand behind Travis's head. Guess he was doing something she liked. That hitch in her breath didn't come from nowhere.

"I wish I didn't have to wait." The little brunette sighed and tickled her titty through her blouse.

Can't disappoint the ladies, now could he? Travis had a mouthful of India and a hand in her crotch, but he had two hands and a brain. Thinking was shutting down, but not so much that he didn't see the wisdom of making Kitty's wish come true. He sidled a hand up the inside of her thigh.

"Ooh, yes," Kitty whispered, her legs falling open. "India, if I cum a lot, will I make as much milk as you?"

"Could be." India's voice came out gritty, like talking wasn't on her mind at all. It shouldn't be, not the way Travis suckled and fingerfucked her.

Yeah, these girls made milk, and if Kitty wanted to lactate buckets, Travis would help that along. Easier since she wasn't wearing any panties either. A man could get used to that. He had a finger for her too, and could he get to where both hands were doing the same thing? In and out of their wet pussies, with some thumb for clits, and…

Hallelujah, India threw back her head and "Aahh!" came out. Her pussy clenched on his fingers. A gush of milk sprayed the back of his throat, more than he'd been suckling. Hot damn, this gal came with milk. Would that happen with both of them?

He curved his fingers up, pressing into her G spot, all nubbly and firm. Just waiting for him to push another orgasm out of it. India rocked back on her fallen log. She gushed at the tit and she gushed at the puss, and the grip on his fingers got tighter.

Perfect, 'cause she was about dry on that side too. Travis waited to let go until her ripples faded. He had two more titties to suck.

"Ready, darling?" Travis asked Kitty, and gave India's thigh a farewell stroke on his way out from under her skirt. Now he had a hand to lower Kitty's blouse, stretching the neckline over her voluptuous boobies. Sparkly peach lace still covered her tits, but he'd learned how to do the one-handed bra-twitch years ago, and her frontloader didn't stand a chance. Not when she had stiff nipples to be uncovered.

Mmm, more milk. He shifted sideways on his fallen log, not caring a whit for the meadowlark trilling from a stump nor the rustle of the hickory leaves. The sun was warm on his back, and so was Kitty's hand. With the other she offered her breast, but—"India, did you want…"

"Let's see what he does." India grinned, like maybe he was passing her test. Or failing it like she wanted. Well, she was in for a surprise, but not until after he'd done some sucking and diddling with her pretty little companion. Kitty's breasts needed his attention, and so did her pussy.

What lovely tits she had, the firm sweet weight below and her nippies poking upward. Stiff nippies, rosy pink, and ready to feed him their milk. Travis latched on to all that titty goodness, getting a big bite of her flesh. With every squeeze of his lips, milk shot out of her hard bud. He got to the cream sooner this time, and she hadn't cum by the time he'd suckled her down to droplets.

"Oh, please don't stop," she moaned, and he wouldn't, not when he had two fingers in her cunt and a titty in his mouth. Didn't have to be the same titty.

So they gave different amounts of milk—this was

firsthand experience. He was glad, in a way—India's bountiful boobies had fed him almost more than he wanted. A full meal, really, and now he had dessert. The sweet cream of Kitty's hindmilk was dwindling away on her second side. And she hadn't cum yet.

Couldn't have that. He could switch off his suckling, put it on that third "nipple" at the apex of her thighs, but he wanted the sweetness of her milk to linger on his tongue. Maybe he'd come back to tease fresh drops out of her later, but for now, he went from suckling for milk to suckling for her pleasure. Put a lot more tongue into it, getting swipes right and left and a little bit of teeth, Just the graze across her flesh, but she shivered and moaned for more.

"Travis… I want…"

"What do you want, sweetheart?" He knew the answer: she wanted cock, thick, leaking cock, jammed right into that pink honeypot.

Maybe India was supposed to get him first, being boss and all, but pretty Kitty's pussy needed to cum.

So too bad. Travis knew he looked fine, all six foot tall and wide shoulders. Six pack of the good stuff on his belly, and eight inches of the better stuff in his BVDs. He stood up to let her get a look at the whole package, and his hands went to his belt. "Is this what you need, darling?"

"Oh!" Her hand flew to her mouth, like he'd said what she daren't. "Yes."

"Let's see what you got there, buddy." India hadn't put her breasts away, oh no she had not, and her smile was the only pale place on her north of her blouse. All that beautiful flesh would be his to fuck here, right after he took care of one horny little brunette.

Travis unhitched his belt, letting the ends fall away with a jingle. Five quick flips of his thumb and his fly opened. Denim could barely contain his dick anyway. He let his cock out, knowing he had enough to make any woman flinch a little, before she leaned forward for a better look.

"Not bad for a white boy." India reached out for a handful. "Let's see what you can do with it."

"More than you think." She'd find out, but right now Travis had to get over and around, because Kitty was looking for a place to get fucked. "Lean over on the log, sweetheart," he advised. "Then your skirt won't get stained."

"Ooh, so thoughtful!" Kitty cooed, but not really, he just wanted that skirt flipped up and out of the way fastest. He didn't need to see a thing beyond her round globes of ass with the juicy secret just below. Open and wet, and missing his fingers, but not the way her coochie would miss eight thick inches when he finally took it away from her.

Wouldn't be for a while though, because he had a trick up his sleeve, or down his jock, or somewhere, and she'd like it…

And he slid right on in. Kitty's cunt welcomed him like an old friend, so hot and slick. Ready to be fucked. He'd go slow, just to let her get warmed up, and then she'd have the ramming of her life. Because he could hardly wait to let her have it.

"Filling you all up, huh, sweetie?" Six inches in, more to go. "I have plenty of cock for you and your pal."

"Promises, promises," jibed India, but Kitty was all Ooh! and Ah! and wiggling ass. She wanted him in, he'd come in.

He could hardly wait to start moving; Travis had to pound that sweet cunt. Picking up speed made her tits sway, and that was a lot of swaying. He leaned over to still their swinging—they made a lovely armful, and he could still reach into her crotch.

Travis planned to make her cum until her knees buckled. If Big Johnson wasn't doing it fast enough, he had another hand, and then he could lean over her ass, feel those bouncy round buns thud against his hips. He slammed into her full speed at last, and she cried out. Well, he wasn't done; he pounded her again and again, getting Oh! And Yes! and "Tra-a-a-a-avis!" out of her.

Hell yeah, he'd pound her into saying his name, he was gonna ruin her for other men. She clenched on him, and he paused. Damn but he liked feeling a woman cum on his cock. Loved the flickering and the gasp of breath and the sudden wetness he could coax out of about half of 'em. Kitty went silent, with his cock stuffed so far in it had to stop her breath. Her clit twitched under his fingers, and her knees buckled. But he'd keep her from falling.

Unless he was gonna fall with her, and he might, the way he came. Her climax triggered his. Goddam yeah, with jizz flying and his nuts pulsing and her pussy getting drowned with cream the way her tits drowned his mouth.

"Want some more, or you want to rest a minute?" Travis asked her.

"I…I gotta catch my breath." Kitty's arms buckled and she lay against the log.

"Big talk," India sniffed.

"You think I'd offer something I can't deliver?" Travis demanded between gasps. "You can have a dose too."

"Like to see you try."

"You want it, bend over so I got a place to put it."

India didn't present her ass until she'd seen him pull out of Kitty, still mostly hard. Travis pinched the base, and his pole stiffened right up. "I got a load or two for you."

"Put your money where your mouth is, pal." India

wiggled her ample buttocks at him. "I ain't felt nothing yet."

"Feel that?" Travis guided his thick rod between her cunt lips. "You want to feel it all?"

Forget slow, forget subtle, forget doing anything but pounding her sassy words out of her mouth from the bottom. He slammed in deep on the first stroke. She was wet enough to take him all, every inch of his wrist-thick cock.

"Oof!" was sweet music coming out of India the doubter. He had enough to pound her with, and her pal, and three more of her companions. He could fuck half the dairy and leave loads in them all. They hadn't seen a man like him.

"Feel it yet?" His hands were steel on her hips. Might leave bruises, but they'd remind her of what it felt like to get fucked. "You're tight enough to feel it all the way to your lungs."

And if she denied being filled, he'd put it in her ass and let her contemplate tightness with her starfish spread to splitting.

"Yeah, I feel it. You gonna do something with it?" Damn but this woman had a mouth. And some moves. Cause India slammed back onto him. She met him half-way, and more than halfway. She took his cock like she wasn't gonna give it back. "Think you got a load for me right after you came?"

"Hell yes I do." Fuck, he was gonna hold off, let her get to where she'd have to beg him for that last touch, but why make her wait to know he meant every word?

Cause she hadn't cum yet. Not with his dick in her pussy like it belonged there. He'd fuck her silly and then when she was reeling, he'd have his second pleasure. And maybe his third.

Good thing India was built sturdy—his every slam shoved her forward and rocked the fallen tree she leaned on. She needed both hands to stay upright under his onslaught. His hairy balls slapped against her clit. He knew damn well she was trying to hold back, and he wasn't having any of that. Not from this gal, who took everything he said as a challenge. She was gonna cum, and she was gonna like it.

He stopped and let her slam back against a groin that weren't there, letting her stumble. One of her hands slipped off the weathered gray log. Travis had her—nope, no face plants into seasoned wood, that would set her orgasm back fifty years. She was off balance though, in every way, and not ready for him to grind his hips around and around, working his balls against her clit. He slapped both hands to her tits, stilling their pendulous swing. Damn but her nipples were hard, and just right for rolling between his fingers. If this didn't bring her off, he'd try his hand, because India *would* admit he'd brought her to the peak.

Just when he thought he'd have to try another way, a cry burst from her. He knew why, he could feel her clenching on his rod. *Yeah. woman, cum all over my dick.* Fuck but she felt good, and why was he holding back now? Travis let himself relax enough to shoot his wad into her hot pussy. Fill her with man cream. Give her what she wanted, that she didn't believe he had.

Damn good thing she was sturdy, because his knees gave a little and she had to hold his weight. Just for a second. And then he was back to pounding her like a big base drum, and getting prettier music.

He had her waist, pulling her back onto his prick. "You need another one?"

"One of yours or one of mine?" she shot over her shoulder. This had to be the most gorgeous smartass he'd ever fucked.

"One for each of us, how about." He'd fuck her into next week, the rate they were going.

"I can do seven before I get irritable, pal, but I don't think you have another one in you." She might have proved herself wrong right then, the way she jammed back on his dick and clenched on purpose. She wasn't letting go, but the joke was on her. Felt good.

"Well then," he allowed, staying still and letting her try to milk him. "You're a woman and all. I'm just a pore ol' boy who runs out of jizz by the fifth orgasm."

"Five! Hah!" She stopped pumping and started laughing, lolling all over that dead tree like he'd told her Conan's monologue. "Guys don't cum five in a row."

"This guy does." He'd prove it, too, starting with another stroke into her cum-slicked pussy. "You want jizz, I am the world's best jizz dispenser."

"Oh hell, I think you were faking that last one." India propped her chin on her elbow and quit trying to fuck-fight him.

"I don't think so, India." Kitty'd been watching, with her hand in her crotch. "His dick is all white and spoozy."

"You're shitting me." India stood up and turned around. Her skirt fell down over her butt, covering the goodies. It'd flip up again real easy, though the sight of her white streaked mound was something he'd miss until that cotton got out of the way. She inspected his dick and ran her fingertip through the white streak on his blue-veined shaft. "Maybe you're not."

"I'm not, but I gotta leave another load in you to equal what Kitty got." Travis smiled grimly, his dick pointing at her crotch. "Each time I shoot a little less. Or maybe you don't need more, since you're such a heavy producer."

"That's how I stay a heavy producer." India bent over and jerked her skirt out of the way. "Do it."

Damn but she had a fine behind. Travis couldn't resist a light slap across her buttock, just for the sound and for the guff. "Does jizz work better in your ass?"

Kitty gasped. The very birds went quiet.

"They'll never find your body." India grabbed his cock with a heavy hand and guided it to her pussy. "You may be more trouble than you're worth, friend. Multiple orgasms or no."

Okay, he'd pushed far enough, maybe too far. "I'm just the right amount of trouble." He slid into her cunt and went back to rocking her world. Hope she got off on death threats or they were back to square one. Course, she'd cum twice so far, she shouldn't complain. "And I'm just the right amount of fun." Yeah with his big boner boning her, maybe a friendly little reach around, she'd be fine.

"Not yet, you ain't." India shoved back hard enough to pinch his balls. Her tits swung hard, slapping together. What a sound. *Slap-a-slap-a-slap,* every stroke made her shake.

A girl could black her own eye that way. Travis grabbed two big handfuls of tit. She'd liked this before, would she like it now, getting her nipples just a little roughed up? Flicked, like he was licking, or tickled? He pulled one, and the log she leaned on went dark with the squirt.

Man, he'd milk her into coming. Pull, pull, squeeze, squeeze, while he fucked her greedy cunt into another orgasm. The job became a misty goal—he just had to dominate this woman's body into doing his bidding. And he did. Fucked her just right, milked her just right, and she went into that quivery, 'gonna fall' state, milking his dick with her climax.

Time to bust another nut. Damn, three into two beautiful women. Travis wished he had another dick to thrust into Kitty. Two women were amazement, two like this, eager and sassy, two was heaven. Two needed him to be some kind of octodick, to fill mouths and hands and pussies, maybe even asses. He reached over to pinch Kitty's nipple. Milk shot out onto his arm, and white ribbons shot out of his dick. He clung to India and gasped. Hot damn. Just. Damn.

She rose, eventually, lifting him up and shrugging him off. Her hundreds of thin braids cascaded down her shoulders, batting him away. Probably a good thing he hadn't grabbed a handful. Next time. When she knew him better. When she liked him a little more. Because whoa, what a grip that would be…

"Hope I did that okay for you." Would she say anything one way or the other? Travis could get a little pissy if she didn't acknowledge his efforts.

"You did okay. That last climax was fine. For me." She shoved her masses of braids out of the way and smoothed her skirt down over her generous, glorious ass. "Not sure you had one."

Travis paused in putting his dick away. "You know, India, I can understand you hearing a lot of crap from men who don't deliver, but I ain't one of them. Wipe your crotch if you think I'm lying."

She snorted. "I hear all kinds of shit, usually from someone who wants something. You want this job—"

"Not as much as I did before I got into a crapslinging match with you," he interrupted. And lied. He wanted a chance at this dairy, for all the other Dairy Maids who didn't have this attitude, and yeah, for a chance to put it to India and have her thank him. "But if I said I can cum five times without losing my stiffy, I damn well can. It's too easy to get bullshit called on you to make lying worthwhile."

"Yeah, it is." She gave him a narrow, slitted glare. "And I'm calling it. Put up or shut up."

All right. Time to make his point with a pile driver. Travis's cock hadn't subsided all that much. Wouldn't be no trouble at all to shoot another little load. He started jacking his cock, which did just what he wanted. What little wilting his Johnson had done would go away real quick, give it a couple of good tugs, staring at two pairs of titties…

India tucked her breast into a navy lace bucket, 'cause that wasn't no mere cup. And Kitty was pulling her blouse up!

"Oh no, you don't." Travis held still. "Didn't say I could do it all alone. I done cum three times, a guy needs a little help." He pointed at the fallen log India'd been leaning on. "You sit here, India. And Kitty, you sit next to her. I gotta have those lovely breasts to look at to keep me in the mood."

Taking Kitty's blouse off put some lead in his pencil for sure. Pull that stretchy neckline down, expose those milksome titties. Travis didn't mind one bit opening her bra again, and Kitty stuck her titties out like a pouter pigeon for him to undress her. Glad someone around here liked him. Travis dared a kiss on her flushed cheek, a kiss he wouldn't dare with India, and a little friendly twiddle to her nipples. Make 'em stand up all perky. "Yeah, there we go. You got to give me a bit of a show, and I'll give you a show."

"I s'pose we can humor you." India leaned back, putting those massive bazzooms on display for him. Well, well, well, her big old nipples on their wide areolas looked like targets to him.

Kitty liked the show idea: she kept playing with her breasts. Her little hands weren't equal to the task of covering up, and that was fine. She liked to play with her nipples. Travis liked that too, and so did John Thomas. That blind boy jutted out of Travis's jeans. Show that doubter what was what.

Travis jacked his cock, still erect. His nuts weren't dry, quite. If he made good on his boast, it wasn't a boast, was it? Show these Dairy Maids what he packed and how he packed it, and what his package could do. His hand flashed up and down his shaft, just the way he liked it when he needed to tear off a quick one. Rolling his balls inside his sack made Kitty say, "Ooh," in that sweet, quiet voice. He'd give her something to ooh over, any minute now.

Damn, but they looked fine! Two succulent white breasts, two luscious black breasts. A sight like that could make a statue cum. Too bad Travis wasn't going to put his spunk where it would do them the most good of all, but he'd make it good for all of them. India would have to admit he was right.

The explosion gathered deep inside. Be there already if he stuck a finger up his butt, but the ladies didn't have to know he liked a little press on the cum button. Save it for a surprise once he'd been hired. Right now they needed to know he could shoot off four times. He got real close, close enough to bump knees with them. Close enough to make them look real careful at the plum purple head of his prick, and remember how good that old boy made them feel. Close enough to make India eat her words without salt.

He jacked harder, faster.

Small ribbons spat from his cockhead. The force and his stroking plopped his jizz right on India's tit. Made pale streaks down her dark skin, looked real fine. If he could open his eyes. He pulsed again, jerking in his own grip. More proof oozed out of his dick, coating his hand.

"Believe me now?" Travis slumped over, too tired to even let go.

"I believe three." India didn't bother to hide her challenge.

"Jesus, woman, are you never satisfied?" If he ever found himself in bed with India, he'd bolster his sex skills with a blue pill or two. Better yet, he wouldn't dickydunk her outside of one of Uncle Horace's situations where she didn't have a say. His cock fucking burned, but he set to tugging once more. She would eat her words yet.

Damn, would he have to resort to poking his prostate? Almost desperate enough to put a hand down the back of his britches, Travis found sympathy in Kitty's eyes, and a last excitement in the palms of her hands. She offered her breasts like a feast, and took one hand away to pull up her skirt. Her pretty pussy spread pink between her open thighs, with streaks of white where his jizz leaked away. Oh, he could tap that! And would again, if he could just prove himself.

With frantic strokes he beat his exhausted meat and only focusing on Kitty's kitty let him find one last climax. He throbbed, and it was good, but small, and only a few drops squished out of his cock. Small splats joined the fluid running down the back of his hand.

Oh!" Kitty cried. "I loved watching you play with yourself." Her eyes were huge, and huger yet when Travis reached out to paint his semen on her nipples. "But not as much as when you put your semen in my pussy."

He tipped Kitty's chin up with one wet finger. "I'll give you all the semen you want, darling. Any time." He turned to India, who threw back her shoulders and accepted his jizz on her nipples. "You, on the other hand, are going to have to be a little nicer first." He pinched her nipple, not hard, but a message. "And there'll be enough to go around for all the Dairy Maids. If you believe me *now?*" Travis couldn't keep the edge out of his voice.

"Oh, I believed you before, but I wanted to see if you could do it." India tucked her titties away. "Kinda impressive."

Travis choked back his frustration. He managed not to yell when he asked, "Think you'll keep me around as hired man then?"

"Might just do that," India said, and kissed Travis square on the mouth.

# The Face-Off

HALF A DOZEN EXCITED Dairy Maids chattered at once about the excellence of their candidates. Three of the four prospects for hired man at the Manley Dairy had passed their private interviews with flying colors, it seemed, and each pair of Dairy Maids insisted their candidate was the only possible choice.

"He's such a gentleman!" and "He's sweet and anxious to please" butted up against "He's got quite the tool and knows how to use it."

Dirk clapped his hands for quiet. "It seems we're no closer to a final choice than we were before." He surveyed his anxious staff. "We have one position to fill, ladies. Brett, Kenny, and Travis all check out on their farming knowledge, have good references for their work ethic, and apparently, they all check out fine with you. We have to narrow the field somehow."

The Dairy Maids got very, very, quiet, though mutinous faces suggested that none would be changing factions.

"Ladies, please join your candidates at the demonstration barn at two o'clock sharp." Dirk Manley had a plan.

———

Kenny tucked into the fried chicken and potatoes au gratin over lunch. Good food and Dairy Maids? Too good to be true. He eyed his fellow job seekers warily over the peach cobbler, while Dirk dominated the conversation. Nervous kid turned out to be Brett, and he must have something more going on than Kenny thought, or he wouldn't still be here, working on a third piece of chicken. Mr. Shit Eating Grin, aka Travis, didn't seem pleased at all to have competition remaining. Too bad.

Two o'clock happened too fast and too slowly, but Kenny and the others met at one of the outbuildings. Dirk had refused to discuss this next part of the interview process ahead of time, but Kenny recognized where they were. He and Taylor had spent a few gentle moments in an intimate situation here. Of course, three risers of seats hadn't been full of Dairy Maids and assorted male guests. Guess word had gotten around.

Three stanchions stood in the open area. Brett's bravado wavered just a bit, and Travis smirked at anyone who'd meet his eye. Kenny took a deep breath. He knew what to do for the Dairy Maid, but the audience left him flummoxed. In front of everyone?

Dirk escorted the three toward the stanchions, and the arena quieted under his booming voice. "Ladies, gentlemen. Thanks you for joining us here today. We have three strapping young men, all anxious to bale hay and clean stalls…" His word got drowned in a gale of laughter. He waited a moment for the mirth to die down.

Dirk wasn't exactly wrong, Kenny did figure to do all those chores too, but the care and milking of Dairy Maids was one hell of a lot more important to him. He could drive a tractor anywhere.

"Our Dairy Maids are having a rugged time choosing, so we're going to have a little bit of a face-off. Those of you who know the Dairy have a pretty good idea of what we'll ask these young men to do. Ladies, we need three volunteers."

The brunette who'd been dumped that morning by Grumpy Applicant popped up from the bleachers. "I will!" She ran to the group to twine her hand into Travis's. Guess she liked the ideas behind that knowing smile.

One of the near women whispered to another, "Of course Rita will."

Her companion just laughed. "And show us what she hasn't got anymore."

"We need two more volunteers." Dirk scanned the group. "Ladies?"

Wouldn't Amy or Taylor stand up? No, those two remained seated, but blew him kisses. Guess private interviews were different than this. Didn't they like him well enough to stand up again? How about India or the others who'd interviewed them this morning? Nope, all seated.

"I just fed…" and "Damn, I wish I wasn't two hours from my next…" explained the lack of assistance.

The busty redhead in dark blue whose sanity had also been questioned by the grouch stood up slowly. "I will." She approached Kenny to introduce herself. "I'm Mindy."

"Hi, Mindy." Kenny smiled down. "Thanks for stepping up. I'll do my best for you."

But no third woman came forward, even when Dirk called again. "Dairy Maids? Someone who hasn't already interviewed one of these fellas?" Taylor and Amy pouted, which warmed Kenny's heart a bit. They weren't getting up because they were disqualified for this morning. "Brett, a moment with you." They stepped aside for low whispers and a handshake. Kenny had time for elation at someone getting eliminated, just like that, which turned to pity for the guy, who slipped away, wouldn't even stay to watch. Guess the only competition now was Travis, whose grin was twice as wide as before.

"Folks, lets get started with our candidates for the dairy's hired man. Gentlemen, given what you've learned so far about the dairy, we're going to ask you to help your companions into the stanchions for a milking, and demonstrate your prostaglandin application technique for us. Fellas, go to."

Dirk sat down to watch, with as much interest as the rest of the audience.

Showtime.

———

Travis watched the young guy leave. Half the competition down already. Another woman was presenting herself for a pounding, and he'd give it to her. Show these folks what a man could do. This little gal would get the fucking of her life. Hope she liked the audience, but hey, she knew better than he did what she was getting into.

Or out of. Like her clothes. Rita stripped pretty good, too, nice slappable ass, trim waist. Titties that looked full of milk, even if her rack wasn't near what the other woman's was. Rita gave milk, he had to fuck her, and that was all Travis needed to know. Rita had her clothes off and was settling herself onto the milking machine. Belly flat to the bench, ass out, tits down.

"Fix the headreast," she demanded, and he would. Settle that stanchion around her head, and oh, hahaha, her wrists were caught. Locked up tight. She wasn't going nowhere until someone let her out. Wonder if she wanted a ball gag too? Or a spreader bar at her ankles? Naw, she had her legs apart already. He'd know if she shaved her pussy here in a minute. Right now he had to fit the pumps over her nipples, all sticking down through holes in the titty buckets. He tickled her nipple, then pinched lightly and pulled. Stiff little thing. Get that milk a flowing. She wriggled and smiled for the attention. Hope the folks in the stand could see how her nipple stretched under his fingers. He pulled again, oops, hard enough to make her squeak. Better put the bottles on. One on each side for the milk. "Ready?"

"Oh yeah!" she breathed, and demanded, "Hit the switch."

Fine with him! Travis flicked the machinery on, and spent a fascinated moment watching her nipples get sucked into the apparatus. They grew huge and shrank back, and in a couple of pulls, white beads started forming and getting sucked into the bottles. Okay, she was letting down, and Travis thought he'd started his first public milking quite successfully. Dribbles of white hit the bottoms of her bottles. Let's see how much milk this little darling could give.

Travis winked at Dirk on his way behind his Dairy

Maid. Oh yeah, the globes of her ass spread lushly apart. There was her pink starfish, which just might need a finger slid in. Heh, yeah, just a fingertip, and she bounced and yipped a little. Not much, guess she liked it. He stuck his finger in a little farther. That got an *ah*.

Didn't one of them say that semen in the ass made even more milk?

Right now though, her pussy spread open, and that looked damned inviting. Shaved, not a hair on those plump lips. Travis ran his thumb up and down her slit. Juicy and getting juicier. He winked at the audience, whose attention was split between him and the other dairy maid, who was just now getting all the way naked. Slowpoke, didn't know shit about efficiency, letting her strip that slow. Travis would give Rita all the prosties she wanted, a couple of guys' worth, and he'd put on a show for the assembled watchers. Uncle Horace had mentioned the show biz aspect to the fucking around here. Travis could perform with the best.

Her milk was squirting away just fine, and her pussy was opening just fine too. He slipped two fingers in. Damn she felt nice. Work that puss, give everyone a thrill, not just her. Making his dick get stiff. He'd take that bad boy out in a minute, give everyone a good look, and then he'd hide it inside that drippy pink cunt. Pound her a while. Make her cum two, three times. See how her tits squirted after that.

That Kenny guy, heh. Not doing a damned thing, best Travis could tell. Just running his hands over that pretty little redhead's creamy skin. Nice ass on her. Big tits, bigger than his Rita's boobies, and giving more milk. Well, some gals gave more than others. Rita was going to milk buckets.

Travis opened his jeans and whipped out his dick, letting everyone get a good look at the eight thick inches he was packing. They wanted a show, he was up to giving it to them. Maybe he was meant for bigger things than a dairy, maybe he ought to be in pictures, the kind that had a bunch of Xs for a rating. But he'd do it live, and they'd like it.

A couple of tugs and a big bead of precum came spoozing out the slit. The droplet fell away, and he was ready to put it to the woman in the stanchion. "Here it comes." He turned slowly, so everyone could see his rod and admire the size. Make sure all the Dairy Maids who hadn't interviewed him were jealous of the two who did. India had that knowing smile on her face, and damned if she didn't sit there licking her lips. Not bad for a white boy, huh. He'd remind her why she kissed him. Except it would be this Rita's pussy getting the juice.

She was open enough, wet enough that only his first stroke went slow. Oh yeah, she was a horny little slut. Didn't even know his name hardly, no two words of hello, big boy, and then spreading. Nope, she just bent over and took it. Travis pushed in, and a gasp from the audience mixed in with her gasp. Yeah, tell 'em you just got filled all the way to your throat with hot man-meat.

Two slow strokes, just to get wet, and Travis cut loose. Hands on her sweet ass, not that she could move, but he liked the way his fingers dented her buttocks while he shoved in and pulled away. Slam that cunt, slam that clit, whap her with his hairy balls and make her cum. She'd love what she was getting, which was a helluva lot more than what that lame Kenny dude was giving his Dairy Maid. Soft words and little tickles over there, and some serious pounding over here. Dumbass.

Rita yipped and yelped, and gasped, and tried to turn around 'cause Travis did get a little too vigorous there, and slammed her head into the headrest. The stanchion squeaked with his every thrust. Ought to oil the damn thing if it was going to get used for fucking.

Rita squealed and went stiff, yeah everything but that pulsing pussy. Orgasm the first. Take that, jackass who barely has his britches down. Travis's dairy maid trembled in the throes of a climax the like of which these folks hadn't seen. Some of the gals had their hands over their mouths, some of the guys had their hands on their dicks. Had to impress Dirk Manley with his handling, though, and Dirk had one of those thoughtful looks going. Probably a higher starting salary.

Travis had a climax going. Just jam in there and spurt

out a good dose of dick milk, paint her pussy with the prostashit that made them lactate. Rita'd just be the first. They'd be lining up for what he was dispensing, and in a couple of minutes and another few strokes, he'd do it again.

That second cum felt damned good, and so did his third. Rita hadn't cum again, but she would, he'd work it so his balls ground against her clit. Fine thought—he had to slap her round ass for the joy of it, just to hear his palm ring against her buttock. She yelped at that, and he felt like smacking her again, make the other side just as pink. Great fuck: she wasn't talking or giving directions or telling him what to do in any way. She was gasping too hard, and if he stuck a finger into her ass to get her ready, well, might not do enough. He had big hands but he had a bigger dick. And she had one tight asshole. Damn, she'd be a vice on his prick, once he got it in there. Maybe with some lube.

Well he didn't have any today, but there'd be other days, so Travis left his finger in her ass and kept on with the fucking. Lot of racket coming out of that stanchion, and a lot of racket coming out of the audience, little comments like "He doesn't know what the fuck he's doing, does he?"

Why didn't they just stop this circus so Kenny could get the hell out with his tail between his legs? Travis could give his dairy maid a couple of shots of jizz too.

Just to keep things even. Cause Kenny was only now working his dick into the little redhead. She was giving a lot of milk. He couldn't see what his dairy maid had given, but he'd check her in a minute.

The pumps hummed and pulsed, and Travis kept the rhythm. Whum, whum, shove, shove, and Rita squeaked again. "OW!" was pretty clear this time. Travis took it a little easier. The audience relaxed a little when he slowed down. Guess they hadn't seen fucking this good.

He had one last trick to show off. He'd come three times, and it was pretty plain he had, his juices coated his cock shiny white. Travis pulled out, and three quick jerks on his cock sent more splats of man cream into her crack. If it did a dairy maid good to get semen in her ass, he'd put it there. Maybe not with his cock this time, but that wasn't much of a show no matter how good it felt. Nope, but he could use his own fuckjuice for lube. Wiping his finger around in the splats got him wet enough to poke back into her asshole, and her pussy was sure wet enough for his dick, and all Rita did was scream and cum. Just quivered and clenched the thick pole in her pussy. She might have fallen if she hadn't been belly down on the milking bench, but her thighs jiggled hard enough to drop her, and her pussy winked on his cock.

Maybe he ought to coax his prick back up, put it in her butt. Give his oohing and ahing audience something to really ooh and ah over.

"That's enough!" Rita yelled.

"Okay, darlin', whatever you say."

Some girls got real testy after sex. A guy couldn't hardly say the right thing, and if she was gonna be like that, he was done. He'd given her what she wanted and now she was gonna bitch? Travis pulled his finger out real slow, and no matter what she was saying, her asshole didn't want to let go. He took his dick out of her too, 'cause he'd had enough. If he slapped her ass now it would be for making her shut up.

But he kept his hand off her butt for now, though after he was hired he wouldn't be so forbearing. He just backed up, strutting a little to show off his barely wilted dick, and tucked it away in his jeans. That ought to convince anyone watching he was the right man for thc job.

———

Kenny glanced at the vigorous fucking going on next to Mindy's stanchion and reminded himself he'd pleased Taylor this morning. His approach then was nothing like this guy Travis's. Kenny'd waited until his interviewer was really relaxed, and then he'd slipped it to her without making a big production out of it. And now he had to do it in public. With people watching. People who'd want a show, but…

Never mind them. His competition was putting on a great show, banging and clanging away, and every Dairy Maid in the audience had her hand over her mouth or her eyebrows meeting her hairline. All while staring at Travis and.... Rita. That was her name, Rita. Kenny didn't want or need that kind of attention, and Mindy, who lay so quietly against the milking bench, seemed aggravated by the commotion.

"Shh, shh, sweetie," Kenny crooned, trying to make some white noise to distract her, calm her. "Shh, shh, just relax." He stroked her lightly, long sweeps along her back and thighs, trying to block out the scene next to them.

Seemed to be working. She settled in, nestling her forehead into the head rest and spreading her knees a little wider. She sighed, and Kenny could only hope she was achieving a milking trance in spite of the racket. He rubbed gentle circles on her sweet bottom, trying to match the tug of the equipment on her breasts. Girl gave a lot of milk. Three ounces a side already. Rita's bottles had half that, even if she'd cum once.

Quit paying attention to the other guy, Kenny told himself sternly. He had a lovely woman who needed his attention. His dick didn't have much trouble focusing on the redhead with the crisp curls on her crotch. Trimmed down nice and tight, not hiding the rosy split of her womanhood. Mindy's pussy blossomed under his thumb, his long, easy strokes bringing her juices. She went shiny with her moisture, and his delving into her depths brought more out.

Keep it gentle, keep it calm, no matter what kind of yipping and clacking went on next to them. The guy was some kind of dervish, but that wasn't what Taylor'd been so happy with this morning. Nope, Kenny would stick with what he knew worked. Any orgasm Mindy thought she missed out on could be made up later.

Her eyes were closed and she seemed nearly asleep, until she wiggled her rump. Spreading her legs a little wider had to be a wordless *Get on with it, fella.* Maybe even a little more personal, like, *Come in, Kenny.*

Sounded good to him, because running his thumb up and down her wet pussy was doing the guy thing to him, audience or no audience. He tried not to pay attention to the men and women sitting on the risers, commenting in low voices on what he was doing. What little registered sounded approving, except when it didn't, and he hoped that was for Travis. New, approving comments like "Nice cock" had to be for him, because he dropped trou right them. Yep, felt good from this side too, stiff and ready to slide into her juicy pussy.

"He doesn't know what the fuck he's doing" had better not be for him, or Amy and Taylor had misled him something fierce this morning. But no, a quick glance at them in the audience and he saw nothing but smiles.

Kenny lined up his cockhead with her hole. Pushing

in, pulling out, nothing too fast, he worked into her. Sliding in on the moisture he'd coaxed out, he didn't move fast or try to rouse her more than she needed to accept his dick. Slow and steady, slow and steady, more soft words and tender caresses for her ripe buttocks. Massaging, not pounding, inside and out.

Might not do enough for Mindy, at least not to make her cum, but hey, this was all about him, so long as he kept to a stately pace. Just feel that sweet pussy around his meat, and treasure the nubbly, slick walls that held him. Whatever Travis thought he had to prove, Kenny wasn't trying to prove. Nope, he'd just fuck this sweet Dairy Maid until he had enough to make him blow. He'd only manage one, unlike Showoff there next to him, but it would be a good one, and Mindy would have nothing to say except "Ah."

Oh, but her skin was soft, and her bottom so lush. Perfect handholds, not too tight. Kenny thrust slowly, savoring each passage through her channel.

A certain commotion next to them made him peek. Guess Rita'd had enough, and Travis was waving his wang around like some trophy. Okay, the guy was hung, but he wasn't paying attention, and doubtful the dairy would remake policy to suit his style. That was fine, that was great. Kenny sheathed himself to the hilt in Mindy's wet pussy and smiled at his audience. Let them share in how good this slow fucking could be.

Another commotion, this time from the audience, with indrawn breaths and murmurs of "Elspeth!" A Dairy Maid Kenny hadn't previously met, all breasts, dark blue skirt, and brunette hair, had entered, leading Brett by the hand. What? Thought he'd been sent packing!

Guess Dirk had sent him after another Dairy Maid. One who stripped with brutal efficiency and let Brett kiss her and settle her and her huge tits into the stanchion. Damn.

He hadn't lost this job yet, and Kenny didn't intend to. Not by making some rube mistake like banging his frustration about more competition into Mindy's pussy. Nope, just fuck her sweetly, fuck her long, and when he spurted, he'd spurt deep and quiet. Fill her with the semen he'd recharged with, the prosty-things she needed, and not disturb her milking trance.

Kenny's world got really small, narrowing down to the woman he filled and his cock traveling in and out of her warm channel. Just letting the climax grow, and erupt, and splash her inside with his cum. His explosion was his own, near silent, spilled deep in her pussy with gritted moans escaping between his clenched teeth. He stayed buried balls deep in her until he started to soften, and refused to think he might be beaten out of his position by a kid.

———

Brett thought sure Dirk Manley was going to tell him to get lost, his Dairy Maids didn't want any part of him. But no, Dirk sent Brett flying up the hill to the farmhouse to collect the Chief Dairy Maid. Elspeth trotted down the hill with him, her eyes alight. "You'll show them, Brett."

And then, before they entered the demonstration barn together, she'd kissed him and said, "Be gentle with me, Brett."

Oh, he'd be gentle all right. If he could get over this cack-handed nervousness, which settling her into the stanchion seemed to make worse. He clipped her into the cuffs and tucked her hair away from her eyes, all while trying not to notice Tough Travis slamming away at his Dairy Maid or Confident Kenny fucking his girl like he didn't have anywhere special to be or anything important waiting for him when he got there.

He'd be gentle with Miss Elspeth, all right, though he wished desperately she was face up and whispering encouragements to him and his dick. The audience seemed all over the place—he couldn't tell if they approved of Travis or Kenny, some seemed to approve, some disapproved, but they all watched with interest while he did his best to follow Elspeth's direction. Brett got her nipples covered up with the pump, and two big bottles attached to catch her milk. Could she really fill those up? Her tits were huge: maybe she could.

He would have liked to do this away from their

watchful eye, but, no choice. He had to. If he wanted this job, and he did, and if he wanted in this lovely woman's vagina. And he did. She was older than he, she'd be more experienced than he, and if she begged for gentleness, it probably wasn't because she'd heard rumors about the size of his dick. Probably because she thought he'd flail all over her and into her and be a general pain in the ass. Well, if she was taking him on as a pity fuck, he'd do his best to make her see she was mistaken.

And if she had heard rumors about the size of his dick, so much the better.

He was going to have to show this audience what he was packing, sooner or later, and he needed a minute to work up to that. Reminding himself he'd fucked two women happy this morning, Brett gathered his courage and rubbed Elspeth's back. Working his way lower and lower, he wanted her to know he was following her instructions. Dirk said Elspeth was the chief dairy maid, so he'd better please her. And right now, even though his cock was stiff, petting her was all he could do. Her two round buttocks got a hand each, and if he swung around behind her, he'd be close to her pussy.

Scary. He could do it, he could fuck her, he'd fucked Chelle and Emily just fine this morning. Glancing up, he caught a glimpse of Emily in the audience. She blew him a kiss. Yeah, he'd given her reason to be pleased, and she'd given him reason to be pleased, and now he had Elspeth presenting herself for his dick. He could do this, Brett told himself, and put his hands to his belt.

The murmurs from the risers sounded encouraging. Brett had to believe they were for him. For the way his hard cock stood away from his body when he dropped his jeans to his knees. For the way his leaky cockhead dripped a blob of precum in a long strand. And for the way he steeled himself to let everyone watch him insert that stiffy into a willing woman, one who didn't want anything from him except gentleness.

Slow, slow, slow, don't blow! Damn but she was warm inside, hot. Slick. For him. For what he'd do to her. Long strokes, all the way in, all the way out. Let 'em watch, they could see he handled himself like a man. Let 'em see he wasn't no virgin any more. Let 'em see how his dick was shiny with a woman's juices. Let 'em see he could give a Dairy Maid what she needed. Wanted. Because this woman who barely knew his name was taking his cock to the hilt. He'd do her right.

Damn but she had a tiny waist. He could nearly put his hands around her, but the swell of her hips made a better hand hold. Brett leveraged himself in deep, and hated to pull out. Except he couldn't go back in less'n he came out a ways. Keep it slow, he'd last long enough to give every man, every woman, and Dirk Manley a good look at him putting it to Elspeth.

The pumps hummed him a rhythm. Every *whum* was

another squirt of milk out of her tits. Every squirt was another stroke in, or another stroke out. The world got real far away, with nothing in Brett's head except the woman under his hands and around his cock, and the milk flowing out of her breasts. He could keep doing this forever.

Or until he couldn't hold his jizz any more, and he stayed plugged into her pussy, spurting and throbbing. Filling her with cream. Busting his nuts into her sweet coochie. Brett leaned over against her firm buttocks. Gentle fucking for her, volcanic explosions for him. Damn. He rocked with his pleasure, and choked on his own breath, trying to be quiet.

He recovered enough to stand up straight, and pull out. Got an ohhh out of the watchers for that. The whole thing was an ohh for him, and if he'd done everything right there'd be more. But right now he'd get his pecker back into his pants.

Brett knelt to check her milk bottles. This Dairy Maid gave a lot of milk. Wow. Close to seven ounces a side and she didn't look done yet. "You're milking real good," he whispered.

Her only sign of hearing was a slight upturn of lips. Her eyes stayed closed, but that almost smile made him happy. Brett watched the milk jet away from her big brown nipples, foaming where it hit the surface. He'd drunk that, this morning, suckling from Chelle and

Emily's breasts, and if he wasn't going to get a taste of Elspeth's milk, he'd watch her produce it.

Finally, amid much muttering from the watchers, he rose. Her nipples hadn't squirted anything but the merest drops for a couple of minutes. She must be done. He cut the pump. Hmm, release the pressure, remove the bottles —close to ten ounces in each bottle, wow! "Are there caps for these?" he asked Dirk.

There were—Dirk produced them from a cabinet, and pointed to a small fridge under the counter. Brett stowed them in the cold. Then he turned back to his sweet dairy maid, and released her from the stanchion. Elspeth sat sleepily on the bench she'd been lying on, and wrapped her arms around Brett's chest. He held her, playing with a lock of her hair.

"I like this one," Elspeth murmured. "Let's keep him."

———

"Let's keep him." Elspeth's words cut Kenny's heart out of his chest. He'd treated his Mindy just as sweetly. Hadn't she produced just as much milk, now also cooling in the fridge?

He wouldn't let her topple, though he wanted to jump up from the bench where he sat with his arm around her, and yell, "Hey! I earned this job!"

Travis hadn't unhitched his Dairy Maid, who'd

stopped giving milk a good twenty minutes ago, and whose bottles were less than half full. The pumps still pulled at her tits. Guess he thought he'd done everything he needed to do, or he was waiting to see what everyone else did, or maybe thinking that she'd benefit from the pumping. Who knew what he thought, except that he was some sort of super-cocksman? But wasn't he supposed to be Kenny's big competition, not that he was. So where did Elspeth get off saying "Let's keep Brett, who's a nervous kid and probably scared of women?"

Except he hadn't looked so nervous just now, and he didn't look scared of Elspeth at all. Not the way he'd fucked her. Real controlled.

Dirk Manley rose from his seat. Dirk had the final say. Didn't he?

Dirk had a quiet question for Mindy, who breathed "Yes" and snuggled harder against Kenny's shoulder when Dirk asked, "Do we keep him?"

Yes! But—there was only one job, and Elspeth said yes to the kid who'd fucked her.

Dirk turned to the audience. "Let's hear it for Brett."

They roared. Damn. Even after what Mindy said? He clutched the pretty redhead more tightly.

Dirk asked them, "What about Travis?" Boos and hisses filled the demonstration barn. "Sorry, Travis, but there's a time and a place, and this wasn't it. Better luck elsewhere."

Travis couldn't have looked more stunned if an anvil had fallen on his head, and started to argue, but the "Sssss" from the crowd made him turn tail. That left— Kenny. His stomach flipped.

"What about Kenny?" Dirk inquired—and the audience exploded.

Okay, he wasn't out of here yet! But— Kenny kissed Mindy for luck, and she kissed back. "Aw!" the Dairy Maids cried.

"Well, fellas." Dirk rubbed his chin thoughtfully. "Looks like your first task around here is going to be getting three well-milked Dairy Maids off to bed for their post-milking naps." He grinned first at one, then the other. "Get Rita unhitched, and don't bother dressing them."

Kenny shut his mouth once he realized it had fallen open, and Brett swallowed real hard.

"Yep, boys." Dirk reached out for a handshake. "Looks like I have two new hired men."

See Lacy Tate's Amazon page for more Manley Dairy stories, coming soon. Because Dairy Maids love to come.

Or join Lacy's blog and be the first to know when there's new stories about the Dairy Maids, their staff, and the visitors, both big and little, who come to drink their luscious milk.

There are plenty of Dairy Maids at the Manley Dairy. Amy, Lara, Heidi, Jordyn, and the rest have milk and stories just for you.

TRAINING
THE
DAIRY
MAIDS
LACY TATE

THE
DAIRY MAID
AND THE
DEPUTY
A Manley Dairy Erotic Story
LACY TATE

THE
DAIRY
MAID'S
DILEMMA
A MANLEY DAIRY EROTIC NOVELETTE
LACY TATE

THE
DAIRY MAID'S
DECISION
LACY TATE

There's lots more sexy, milky stories at the Manley Dairy.

Buy at Amazon or read on Kindle Unlimited.